CIA

UNRAVELLING MYSTERIES OF USA'S FIRST LINE OF DEFENCE

N. CHOKKAN

PRABHAT
PRAKASHAN

Published by
PRABHAT PRAKASHAN PVT. LTD.
4/19 Asaf Ali Road,
New Delhi-110 002 (INDIA)
e-mail: prabhatbooks@gmail.com

ISBN 978-93-5562-719-3

CIA – UNRAVELLING MYSTERIES OF USA'S FIRST LINE OF DEFENCE
by N. Chokkan

Edition
First, 2024

Price
₹ 300 (Rupees Three Hundred Only)

Printed at
Sita Fine Arts, Delhi

Author's Note

The world of espionage has captured the imagination of the public for generations. Yet much of what occurs behind the cloak of intelligence agencies remains hidden in mystery. The Central Intelligence Agency (CIA) has been at the forefront of both covert operations and controversy since its founding in 1947. Its mission encompasses intelligence gathering and analysis related to national security threats, as well as undertaking covert actions authorized by the President.

As a key component of the United States intelligence community, the CIA has played a pivotal yet often unseen role in some of the most significant geopolitical events of the 20th and 21st centuries. From infiltrating Nazi ranks during World War II to attempts to undermine Fidel Castro's regime during the Cold War, the Agency frequently operated with unclear boundaries between diplomatic and clandestine activities. Public perception of the CIA ranges from vilifying to sensationalistic, magnified by Hollywood portrayals. But piecing together declassified records points to an organization devoted to protecting American interests, while walking an ambiguous moral line in carrying out its directives.

Recent decades have seen the CIA transform to address the new paradigm brought on by global terrorism and technological shifts. Both covert and collaborative efforts across over 130 countries now focus on disrupting threats and violence from extremist groups. The Agency has also reinvented its analytics using leading-edge data science to inform national security strategy.

The chapters ahead provide an inside look at the CIA's evolution, scrutinizing both accomplishments and controversies. The events and evidence unfold through the lens of insiders and policy analysts. The assessment casts new light on the outsized role this agency has assumed in guiding geopolitics from the shadows. Both novices and scholars of security affairs will find ample information to make their own judgments on the necessity and ethical dilemmas inherent to intelligence work. By evaluating the CIA in full context, we come closer to balancing its mandate with the ideals of transparency and accountability in an open democracy.

❑

Contents

1
Hit

It was the wee hours of 3:30 in the morning.

The American Navy witnessed a strange happening during that hour. The Pearl Harbour patrol sent a message that a submarine was moving near their border. Higher officials immediately woke up from their slumber.

It was during the Second World War. Although America was not involved in the war directly, it was required to be always on alert since it was not known when and where the next attack might be.

When a submarine was spotted suddenly, the Americans went on super alert mode. *To which country does the submarine belong? What are the weapons hidden inside? Is it a solo submarine or are more on their way?*

They gathered an army secretly during dawn. *We must find that submarine, only then the mystery can be solved.*

It was an attack which the Americans did not even anticipate. The entire fleet of the US Navy was stationed at Pearl Harbour. But they never imagined that they would be attacked. The major surprise in the attack was their 'attacker'—Japan!

Everybody was nervous. It took four hours for them to realise that they were surrounded by enemies on all sides through sea, land and air. The enemy army made use of their confusion and started attacking. Numerous warcraft surrounded Pearl Harbour within seconds and started to attack. It was an attack which the Americans did not even anticipate. The entire fleet of the US Navy was stationed at Pearl Harbour. But they never imagined that they would be attacked.

The major surprise in the attack was their 'attacker'—Japan!

When you look at the world map, the distance between the US and Japan might appear to be a lot. But since the world is round, both the nations are neighbours. If you board an illegal immigrant ship in Japan, you can reach the US border through the Pacific Ocean without any hindrance.

Japan took the same route. Six aircraft carriers, hundreds of aircraft within, battleships and submarines formed a huge army and started from Japan. They halted at a place a few miles from Pearl Harbour without anybody's knowledge. They started their attack on the early morning of a Sunday.

What is the reason behind the Pearl Harbour attack? How did the tiny nation of Japan have the courage to attack the US? What are the after effects of this attack? The answers for these questions are not needed for this book. What we need to look at is that Japan had attacked the US unexpectedly.

The hit was not even small; it was a massive hit. The US Army was not prepared for this attack and was resting at Hawaii. Japanese aircraft started to bomb innocent public and on the other side, started demolishing American warcraft.

There was heavy damage caused to the US before they realised the impact and started to defend themselves against the Japanese forces. 7 December 1941 became a shameful date in the American history.

The attack lasted no more than ten hours. The Americans were terrified in that time. No one could believe that such a tiny nation which can be easily ignored in the world map made such an efficient attack on the mighty US.

The US entered the world war after that. It dropped atom bombs on Japan later. But how could they not anticipate such an attack in the first place?

The attack lasted no more than ten hours. The Americans were terrified in that time. No one could believe that such a tiny nation which can be easily ignored in the world map made such an efficient attack on the mighty US. The US entered the world war after that. It dropped atom bombs on Japan later. But how could they not anticipate such an attack in the first place?

The major worry of America during that period was the above question. Their superpower image would hold good only until other nations considered them as a mighty power. If the other countries got to know that anybody could catch them off guard, like Japan, their image would take a beating.

America started to analyse where they were lagging and how did they fail to predict such an important matter. When they compiled the results of this analysis, they faced a shock more severe than the Japanese attack.

Japanese officers were talking to the American government from before the Pearl Harbour attack. But there was an urgency in their approach after November 1941. It meant that Japan was making arrangements for war and were friendly with America, both at the same time. They were involved in secret activities without letting out their real intention.

A Japanese minister had spoken that a smooth decision should be reached between the US and Japan before November 29. US did not understand his warning. "The situation will go out of control after that."

In the beginning of December, Japanese embassies all over the US received an order: "Keep the most important documents and destroy everything else."

Japanese officers were saying that war could be avoided after that. A few code words were repeated in their conversations. Several submarines disappeared from the US radar suddenly. Unconfirmed information that the Japanese were rehearsing for a secret attack was passed. The most appalling news is that the US knew all these before the Pearl Harbour attack. Yet they could not foresee that Japan was planning to attack them.

America's weakness was the same. Isn't it stupidity to sit idle even after having all the information?

When they started to analyse, the US realised something clearly. Trusting military intelligence alone is not enough in such situations. A separate intelligence department is required to analyse and report external affairs.

If the US had such an intelligence wing in 1941, they would have noticed the Japanese activities. They would have warned the government on the upcoming danger. They would have avoided such a shameful event.

There was a six-year gap between the Pearl Harbour attack and CIA's inauguration. But only after the attack, did the US realise that they needed such an agency.

❑

2
Genius Army

'Wild Bill'

This was the nick name given by his friends to William Joseph Donovan. Donovan was not a gang leader. He was an educated solicitor, military officer and an intelligence expert. Despite all these identities, the name 'Wild Bill' stuck with him for a reason.

Donovan crossed several hardships in his life and reached a certain position. He disliked his enemies intensely. He was highly patriotic and did not hesitate to oppose anybody for that. He was a wild person who considered America's enemies as his own enemies and charged against them. In general, solicitors talk a lot. But Donovan was against talking, he was more action-oriented rather than shooting out plenty of words.

During the First World War, William Donovan guided his battalion and led them well. He won several distinguished military awards for his service. Donovan went back to his law career after the war. But the US government was not ready to leave him. He was given several important responsibilities and posts after that.

That was the period when Donovan developed interest in the intelligence activities. He realised that numerous new enemies were emerging all over the world against the US. He emphasised to the US government that they need to be monitored regularly and controlled.

Unable to handle his nagging, the American government started to consider Donovan's recommendation. It decided to form an intelligence department to find out about the activities of other nations during the war, their strengths, which country planned to invade which country and other important war information.

The Second World War started in that period. Although America did not participate in it directly, Donovan warned that somebody might poke them with some unwanted activities. He recommended creating a separate intelligence agency to identify and avoid such dangers.

Unable to handle his nagging, the American government started to consider Donovan's recommendation. It decided to form an intelligence department to find out about the activities of other nations during the war, their strengths, which country planned to invade which country and other important war information.

Donovan's arguments were accepted in paper. America decided to create a department which acts only during the war period and not as a permanent force. Although Donovan was not completely satisfied with this, he consoled himself to work with what was available and started his arrangements.

The American government looked at the intelligence department just like any other government department. It involved very few in intelligence activities, just for a formality. Those few agents were not provided with sufficient comfort and arrangements. When asked for extra budget, they were either refused or ignored.

An intelligence wing named Coordinator of Information (COI) was started in July 1941. This group ran under the direct control of the US president.

The intelligence tasks given to Donovan during the initial days were challenging. Most of them revolved around a single person—Hitler. Hitler fever had affected the entire world then. Although Hitler did not directly provoke America, the Americans wanted to know if Hitler would be a threat to them or not.

Donovan was given this task. *Was Hitler's Nazi army powerful? What effects might Hitler make in other nations including Britain? Do we have any immediate or long-term danger due to him? Is Hitler a friend or a fiend to the US?*

Donovan had several questions like these and travelled around the world. Although spying the world outside their military was new to the US, Donovan and his intelligence officers did their job well. America periodically received information about Hitler's actions. Based on that information, US took its consequent political steps.

But, even after that, unlike Donovan's expectation, the US did not give enough importance to its intelligence activities. The reason was that they were not directly involved in the war. The American government looked at the intelligence department just like any other government department. It involved very few in intelligence activities, just for a formality. Those few agents were not provided with sufficient comfort and arrangements. When asked for extra budget, they were either refused or ignored.

Apart from this negligence, the information gathered by Donovan and other spies were not even utilised properly. The agents just read them like a morning newspaper and disregarded the information.

Donovan was frustrated on looking at these activities. He was upset that no one including the American politicians, rulers, officers or public understood the importance of having an intelligence wing. But Donovan did not give up his efforts in any situation. He continued to emphasise the importance of improving the strength of the intelligence wing and to give more credit for their discoveries.

In this situation, Japan decided to poke the US. They performed a huge action at the US harbour. The Pearl Harbour attack was a huge shock to the US. It shattered the confidence that it was safe and nothing could affect its well-being. It was understood that anybody could demolish US with a little extra effort.

Donovan wanted to make use of that fear in a positive direction. He asked, "We have been talking about this for a long time. If we had a strong intelligence agency, would we have faced such an attack?"

The American government considered Donovan's words with respect for the first time. It too understood that strengthening the intelligence department was important.

Within a year of the inauguration of the COI inauguration, another intelligence agency named Office of Strategic Services (OSS) was formed following the military order. William Donovan was the leader of this agency. But even then, the government was not ready to completely hand over control to Donovan.

"Japan attacked us today and some other country might attack us in the future. America has several enemies all over the world. If we have to protect the US from such an attack in the future, we should have eyes all over the world. We must analyse even a small movement and find out if that might affect us," said Donovan.

The US entered the Second World War at this time and hence the danger was doubled. The COI was strengthened to manage the situation. But Donovan said that COI was not enough for the task and another special intelligence system was needed. The American government accepted Donovan's request as it had not completely recovered from the shock of the Pearl Harbour attack.

Within a year of the inauguration of the COI inauguration, another intelligence agency named Office of Strategic Services (OSS) was formed following the military order. William Donovan was the leader of this agency. But even then, the government was not ready to completely hand over control to

Donovan. So, it announced clearly that OSS was a temporary agency created just for the purpose of the world war.

Donovan's OSS was the foundation for the future CIA. Donovan is called the Father of CIA. During Donovan's period, the intelligence task was considered to be done only by geniuses. Only those who had graduated from the top universities of the US were admitted into the OSS; only they were given important roles.

Moreover, the US already had a police force and the FBI (Federal Bureau of Investigation) to handle internal affairs. It issued an order that the OSS had to only deal with foreign affairs to avoid any power conflicts with their internal forces.

Donovan did not bother with these politics. He had got an intelligence agency with more powers just like he wished. He believed that if he could utilise the chance well, it could be changed into a permanent agency. The best intelligence experts were gathered from the American Army and other departments for OSS. These experts and other juniors who were trained by them started their foreign intelligence tasks. This group analysed each activity done by each of their enemy nations. They compiled everything including their army strength, future plans, possible threats and sent them to their government.

Donovan's OSS was the foundation for the future CIA. Donovan is called the Father of CIA.

During Donovan's period, the intelligence task was considered to be done only by geniuses. Only those who had graduated from the top universities of the US were admitted into the OSS; only they were given important roles.

The same situation prevailed during the initial stage of CIA too. The fact that there is no connection between being a topper in the class and spying was understood by them at a later stage.

In any nation, politicians and governments do not favour geniuses. American rulers of Donovan's period were worried about OSS. They were hesitant to provide additional powers to them. They were tentative that if more independence is given to OSS, they might grow into a huge power which might control the government. Hence, most of the officers looked at the growth of the intelligence wing with caution.

The Second World War had ended at this time. They quoted it and dissolved OSS. It was announced that internal departments would take care of the responsibilities of OSS too.

Donovan was exasperated. Who said that all the dangers to America had subsided once the war was completed? Isn't being cautious always good for the country's safety? If Donovan was born in our country, he would have got the name 'Vikramaditya'. In spite of all the setbacks, he continued to push the government with all his files.

"Hello leaders, kindly listen to me. Intelligence is not something that is necessary for just this time. We can know about the happenings around us only through it. Only then we can protect ourselves. It is sheer stupidity to dissolve the intelligence agency once the war is over. Kindly think with long-term benefits in your mind. You will understand the truth in my words."

Donovan continued his efforts. But no one was ready to accept that the US needed an intelligence agency during the peaceful time after the war.

In general, Donovan hated America's enemies. But in that situation, one of the enemies of America helped his cause.

That enemy was the Soviet Union!

❑

3
Beyond the Border

Consider two people who are ready to get into a nasty fight. Their animosity lasts from several decades. They have challenged each other several times both directly and indirectly. Both have planned how to react based on each one's supporters, their strengths and their abilities. In this situation, if one among them suddenly enters a room and locks himself, what will his opponent do?

The US was in such a confusion then. They considered the Soviet Union as the challenger for their influence over the world, but the Soviet Union had shut their doors tight. It didn't mean that they had deviated from poking the US. They continued their notorious tasks in utmost secrecy.

Nobody from outside knew anything about what was happening within the Soviet Union. The then ruler of the country, Stalin declared that there was no need for any outsider to know about the happenings within their country.

Several nations were curious to know what was happening behind the closed doors. They called the Soviet Union the 'Iron Curtain'. But the nation did not bother with the comments and continued their fortification.

During the Second World War, the US dropped atom bombs on Japan and caused heavy destruction. All the world nations including America realised the real power and perils of nuclear weapons during the Hiroshima–Nagasaki incidents.

It was not just curiosity which triggered the US to know what was happening in the Soviet Union, but it was a necessity for them. The reason was that whatever the Soviet Union did, its effects would fall upon the US.

During the Second World War, the US dropped atom bombs on Japan and caused heavy destruction. All the world nations including America realised the real power and perils of nuclear weapons during the Hiroshima–Nagasaki incidents.

This caused humanitarian cries to ban nuclear research and to stop producing nuclear weapons on the one side. On the other side, many countries started to consider nuclear weapons, thinking that they would keep them safe.

It was as if the bombs dropped by the US had fallen on their own heads. In general, the Soviet Union was strong in their scientific research. Now, the US themselves had showed them the capability of nuclear weapons.

So, the US wanted to obtain information about the Soviet Union. *Are they manufacturing nuclear weapons? If yes, how far have they progressed? What is their strength? How and where have they gathered their army? What new weapons have they found?*

Americans understood the extent of Donovan's cries that intelligence is required even during the non-war times. They formed a new intelligence agency named Central Intelligence Group (CIG) in January 1946. Harry S Truman was the US president then.

The Soviet Union did not leave a peeping gap and strengthened their security measures. Several restrictions were made for foreigners to enter their country. Even if they entered, they made sure that no secret was leaked out to them. If they suspected somebody of being a foreign spy, they made sure to lock them up for life.

America's curiosity increased due to these activities. They decided that unless they knew about what was happening inside the Soviet Union, they were not safe.

Americans understood the extent of Donovan's cries that intelligence is required even during the non-war times. They formed a new intelligence agency named Central Intelligence Group (CIG) in January 1946. Harry S Truman was the US president then.

Later, CIG was renamed into CIA (Central Intelligence Agency). 18 September 1947 is celebrated as the birthday of the CIA.

Since the day CIA was formed, certain aspects were declared to be their primary mission:

- Undertaking actions against America's enemy nations.
- Undertaking actions supportive to America's friendly nations.
- Making sure not to leak out the fact that America was funding for these actions.
- Spreading America's opinions and policies in foreign countries.
- Extending direct/indirect support to opposite groups in America's enemy nations.
- Helping nations/groups which are anti-communism.

Although the list was long, everybody knew the real mission of the CIA. It was to draw a border around the US and to do any action outside it, but the people inside the border should not be affected.

America sent an indirect warning through this to all the countries' rulers—*Do you accept our policies? Do you believe that we are superior to everybody? Good, we will make sure that no harm nears your rule!*

Similarly, the Soviet Union and other nations which support communism, and their rulers were added to the US enemy list. It was an unwritten rule in CIA to do anything to overthrow the government of these countries.

But wasn't CIA formed to ensure the US's safety? What is the relation between overthrowing governments and American safety? If a country supports Soviet Russia, it means that their influence is increasing. How can the US be at peace in a world where communism is rising?

America said that they did everything to safeguard people of the world from the monster of communism. But in truth, they did not like a group or a government, anywhere in the world, which was against their policies.

America said that they did everything to safeguard people of the world from the monster of communism. But in truth, they did not like a group or a government, anywhere in the world, which was against their policies.

At the very beginning, they tried to crush their external enemies. But this earned them an image as the 'guardian of the world'. The power which CIA had during their initial stages was less. But they gained strength over the years, both knowingly and also secretly.

Until today, the US has never revealed the actual budget allocated to CIA or how it is spent. In addition to that, the activities that CIA agents and officers are involved in are also kept as secret.

An easy reason for this is that, this information cannot be revealed. Starting from the day the CIA was formed, it was fulfilling their responsibility to change the thinking of the entire world in support of the US.

What if somebody opposes it? What if they refuse to accept US dominance?

According to CIA, both are the same. CIA will do anything to overpower anybody who refuse to accept US or who consider US as their enemy.

Anything includes everything. Their agents were given complete freedom in this aspect. They start by spreading anti-government comments in their country. When internal conflicts occur due to these comments, they find anti-government groups and supply them with money and weapons. If possible, they provide indirect military support or make the prominent people in the government disappear.

Americans did not realise that a group which was formed to spy on other nations and provide their report was morphing into something big. Either they did not notice it or they started to enjoy their actions.

CIA's power was rapidly spread throughout the world with the American government's blessing!

❑

4
Murky Ponds, Swollen Fish

During the Second World War, Benito Mussolini was the one among very few who supported Hitler. The Italian dictator Mussolini was captured and killed during the war long before Hitler was defeated. Only after his death, democracy bloomed in Italy and people started to breathe in peace.

Three parties were prominent in Italy's political field during that time; the Republic Party named DC (Christian Democrats), Italian Socialist Party (PSI) and the Italian Communist Party (PCI).

During Italy's first public election, all the three parties contested individually. Not one party got the majority. So, the three parties joined together to form a coalition government. The Republic Party led this alliance. The two other parties held a few cabinet posts.

This coalition government did not last long. Due to several political issues, the Republic Party removed PCI and PSI from the government. The irritated PCI and PSI made a separate alliance and started pressurising the Republic Party.

What will happen when two of three equally powerful parties unite? Their strength will overpower the third party. The same happened in Italy. Opposition parties gained more power than the ruling party. This led to several political instabilities.

There is no relation between Italy's election and the US. But the US came to a decision that if the Republic Party is defeated in the election, that might be dangerous to them. The reason was that the two parties which opposed Republic Party favoured communism. It was rumoured that the Soviet Union was supporting the two parties in the background.

In this situation, another public election was conducted in 1948. The Republic Party contested alone in that election. The other two parties formed an alliance and contested together. Republic Party was surely expected to fail in the election.

In that situation, CIA decided to interfere in the election.

There is no relation between Italy's election and the US. But the US came to a decision that if the Republic Party is defeated in the election, that might be dangerous to them. The reason was that the two parties which opposed Republic Party favoured communism. It was rumoured that the Soviet Union was supporting the two parties in the background.

If the two-party alliance won the election, a communist government would be formed in Italy. Would the US tolerate it? It decided to enter the field and make the pond murky.

In whichever direction the public turned in Italy, the media was blaring that communism was a giant demon waiting to gobble up the public. People didn't know who was behind this campaign. But their suspicions were aroused on hearing the same facts repeatedly. They started to wonder if communism was really a boon or a bane.

But the election was to be conducted in Italy and the voters were Italians. Even if any problem arose, that would be Italy's internal problem. It would not be good for the US to interfere in it.

So, the US sent its CIA agents to Italy. They could do anything behind the screen. If their action led to a scandal, the US could move away saying they had nothing to do with it. The only mission given to the CIA was to make the Republic Party win at any cost. They made a perfect to-do list to achieve their goal and started towards it.

Their first task was to spy and find out who had more support in which region. CIA came to know that the Republic Party was pushed to the second place in almost all the regions. Following this realisation, an anti-campaign was started through magazines and radios at great cost. The notices, books and speeches released by the CIA showcased the negative effects of the communist rule.

"My dear Italians, if you are planning to vote for PSI or PCI, kindly think again. Do you know how the communist rule has affected people throughout the world? You won't allow your Italy to be grabbed by communist monster hands, would you? Think before you act, since your future is in your hands."

Philippines got their freedom after the Second World War and they had a government which was pro-USA. So the US was providing them monetary support. In return, they used Philippines as their military base.

The truth or lack of it in this campaign was not important. They repeated it innumerable times. In whichever direction the public turned in Italy, the media was blaring that communism was a giant demon waiting to gobble up the public. People didn't know who was behind this campaign. But their suspicions were aroused on hearing the same facts repeatedly. They started to wonder if communism was really a boon or a bane.

CIA moved to their next step immediately. They targeted Italy's communist leaders after that. They placed blame on some leaders and produced evidence for all of them. Most of the 'evidence' was forged by CIA. But Italians did not know about that. Communism was new to their nation. They decided not to take a risk by choosing them. All the Italian socialist and communist votes turned towards the Republic Party.

The Republic Party which was struggling when the election was announced, had a massive victory in the election. Almost half of the total votes submitted went to them. The Republic Party rule was established in Italy just as the US wanted. The communist party which went down then, could not manage to rise up to power in Italy. CIA's first important foreign mission was completed successfully.

After one and a half years, CIA played the same Italy drama. The country under their radar was Philippines.

Philippines got their freedom after the Second World War and they had a government which was pro-USA. So the US was providing them monetary support. In return, they used Philippines as their military base.

Communists blocked their path there too. The military wing of the Philippines communist party called Hukbalahap, rebelled against their government which was supporting the US. This led to protests and riots throughout Philippines. The Philippines government watched with concern as the rebels gained public support gradually.

Communists blocked their path there too. The military wing of the Philippines communist party called Hukbalahap, rebelled against their government which was supporting the US. This led to protests and riots throughout Philippines.

Philippines asked the US for support to oppress their protests. The US gave this task to the CIA. The same Italian screenplay was telecast again in Philippines. "Communists are against people. Will you support them?"

Wasn't evidence needed for these claims? The CIA and Philippines Army planned and executed some violent attacks and put the blame on communists.

Apart from campaigns, they had a few other important matters in Philippines. They brought in the weapons and equipment needed for the local army and gave them the training needed to use them. The Philippines Army was made ready to handle the internal clashes.

Philippines had its public election in 1953. CIA started its work in making the pro-US party win. The anti-communism campaign was in full speed. Complaints were made against their enemies with evidence. At the end, the party which the US favoured won the election and formed the government.

Iran faced a political change in the same year and CIA was behind that too. Mohammed Mossadegh was chosen to be their leader in Iran. Some of his political strategies were not liked by the Western countries. Britain decided that his rule could not be continued and entered the field. They asked the CIA for support.

The CIA searched for and found those who did not like Mossadegh's actions and opposed his way of thinking. Anyone who was against Mossadegh was encouraged to raise weopons against him. Several youngsters were given monetary support and weapon training. They spread hatred towards Mossadegh among the Iranian people.

Bringing down Mossadegh was their primary mission. The next step was to find a compliant person and make him the ruler. Several secret activities were made to achieve both their goals. The CIA searched for and found those who did not like Mossadegh's actions and opposed his way of thinking. Anyone who was against Mossadegh was encouraged to raise weopons against him.

Several youngsters were given monetary support and weapon training. They spread hatred towards Mossadegh among the Iranian people. They entered into fights with the Mossadegh supporters. Through these activities, people revolted just like

CIA expected. The US utilised the situation and caught many fishes in the murky pond. They trained several other rioters and ballooned the problem.

In August 1953, the rebels overpowered the government. Prime Minister Mohammed Mossadegh was arrested and sent to prison. The government which the US and CIA favoured was formed in Iran.

The same thing happened in Guatemala the next year. The government which supported communism or which was thought to be favouring communism by the US was overthrown by the CIA. The person who was brought down by the CIA was Jacob Arbenz Guzman. He came to power in Guatemala in 1951 and was making several reforms in the country. Arbenz Guzman's reforms showed him as a communist. The US noticed it and was alerted.

That was the period when communism had started to spread not only in Europe but also in the US. The US wanted to remove this threat in its initial stage and was taking several actions towards it. Everybody looked like a communist to them. Starting from officers and politicians, they found writers, artists and cine artists who were considered to support communism and blocked them. Hollywood's popular comedian, Charlie Chaplin, too was one among those who was barred entry to the US on these charges.

There is no wonder that those who suspected Charlie Chaplin, suspected Arbenz Guzman to be a communist. The US guessed that he was working along with Soviet Union and decided to throw him down from power.

The US which was adamant in not allowing communism to grow in faraway countries like Italy and Philippines did not like a communist-supporting party to rule in Guatemala which was right under their nose. The fear of what would happen if Arbenz united with the Soviet Union made them take some extreme steps.

Moreover, a few American companies which were affected by Arbenz's rule tried to bring him down . The American government was made to involve in the situation by them.

CIA named the plan to overturn the Arbenz Guzman government as 'PBSuccess'. The formula which was used and found successful in Iran was used again. Find out the rebels who oppose the government, support them, anti-campaign, attacks, rebellions, confusions, riots and then new government!

CIA's plan worked perfectly. They found a few local groups which did not like Arbenz's rule and gave them all the support they needed. They gave them their blessings and sent them into the field.

On the other side, America gave political and economic pressure to Guatemala. Anti-communism campaigns were also in full swing. Guatemala's small government couldn't manage CIA's attacks from all directions. CIA achieved its goal using a few hundred local rebels.

Arbenz Guzman was forced to resign his post.

CIA gained confidence following its consecutive victories in two countries—Iran and Guatemala. They started to search for more communist supporters (i.e., anti-Americans).

Cuba came under the radar then. A revolutionary government under the leadership of Fidel Castro was ruling the country. CIA decided to overpower him just like the other communist rulers. That decision might have been made at an inauspicious time. The Cuban serpent which coiled around the legs of the CIA then remained as a black mark in the history of CIA till today.

❑

5
Naive Agents

In the world-famous comedy magazine *Mad*, a popular cartoon series named 'Spy Vs Spy' was published. Two spies were featured in it. One was a black spy and the other a white spy. Both were from two different countries. Both try to steal the opponent's secret and attack the other person.

In general, spies are considered as geniuses. But this cartoon series revealed that in order to overpower the other person, the spies could act foolish at times. This 'Spy vs Spy' cartoon series with only pictures and not a single dialogue was welcomed by its fans in many countries.

But, do the agents act in such a foolish way in real life?

Antonio Prohias, the artist who created the 'Spy vs Spy' characters never gave a direct answer to this question. But in his birth nation Cuba, several spy comedies which would overpower his humorous cartoons have taken place.

The screenplay, dialogues and editing was by none other than the CIA!

The mission of the CIA was not to direct a comedy movie in Cuba. But all the actions which they took against Cuba's ruler Fidel Castro failed miserably. Such was the support Castro had among his people. His army and the security people predicted all the activities of CIA and counteracted them.

> *The CIA tried hard to kill Fidel Castro, but in vain. Not once or twice, but the CIA had tried and failed 638 times to kill Fidel Castro. No other leader in the history would have faced so many attacks on his life!*

The CIA tried hard to kill Fidel Castro, but in vain. Not once or twice, but the CIA had tried and failed 638 times to kill Fidel Castro. No other leader in the history would have faced so many attacks on his life!

Do not ignore them as rumours. In an article written by the eighty-year-old Fidel Castro, he himself has confirmed that CIA/US had made several attempts on his life. In addition to that, CIA's secret documents are being gradually released to the public in the recent years. A book, *CIA Targets Fidel* has been released on the methods CIA employed in their attempt to kill Fidel.

If you expect a James Bond kind of action in this book, you will be disappointed. Comedy scenes are scattered throughout the book and the reader might wonder if such naïve plots can even be formulated.

A few examples:

- Castro is fond of Cuba's Havana cigar. Hide some explosive materials inside one of his cigars, he would light it and then 'bamm'!
- One of Castro's hobbies was to swim underwater for a long time. Apply poison on his swim wear, and the poison would spread to his body when he wears the swimsuit. His body will be paralysed and he will drown.
- Smuggle a poison dart through a CIA agent. If he pricked Castro with the dart, the poison would take care of the rest.

At the end, as a final attempt, CIA approached the Mafia. CIA hired them to finish off Castro through some way. Their attempt too was futile. Cuba's intelligence department captured Mafia agents armed with guns and also carrying poison on their bodies. CIA did not know what to do next when Fidel Castro was safe and sound in spite of all their efforts. They just dropped their mission and had to wait until he died of natural causes.

- CIA bribed one of Castro's girlfriends and sent poison pills through her. If she managed to mix those pills in Castro's food without his knowledge, the deed would be done.
- Spray bacteria-mixed poison on his handkerchief. Wouldn't he ever use his handkerchief to blow his nose or to wipe the sweat?

Although the list of CIA's attempts on Fidel Castro's life extends to a mile, all the attempts ended in failure. Nobody who was sent by CIA was able to reach Castro. Castro's security was strictly maintained to such an extent.

At the end, as a final attempt, CIA approached the Mafia. CIA hired them to finish off Castro through some way. Their attempt too was futile. Cuba's intelligence department captured Mafia agents armed with guns and also carrying poison on their bodies.

CIA did not know what to do next when Fidel Castro was safe and sound in spite of all their efforts. They just dropped their mission and had to wait until he died of natural causes. Everything CIA did with respect to Castro was a failure. They failed miserably to overthrow his government during the initial days.

That was a huge mistake by CIA. They planned to execute the same plan in Cuba, which they had in other countries. They thought of bringing down Castro and finding a puppet to rule the country . But they did not think well before starting their action. Their plan which had bagged them victory in other nations failed in Cuba. The reason for the failure is the public support Castro had among his people. The US and CIA failed to predict it.

Americans think that the entire world think just like they do. They cannot think otherwise. They believe that they don't like communism, so everybody around the world also does not like communism. Those who rule a country against their policies are to be removed from power. America's adamancy did not bear fruit in Cuba. Cubans considered Castro as their true leader. The CIA did not understand that and tried to disturb Cuba and fish in it.

John F Kennedy was the president of the US during that period. CIA executed all their Cuba plans with his blessing. Their initial plan was to execute a direct weapon attack on

Cuba. But it might cast a black mark on their name in the world. So they decided to take the hidden route as usual.

Their plan did not have any major change—finding local groups which have enmity towards Castro and want to gain power, gathering all of them and providing them all the help they needed, and starting a revolt. A place called Bay of Pig was chosen to start their revolt against Castro. Later, the plan was also named as 'Bay of Pig' invasion.

As usual, CIA found a few rebels in Cuba. They prepared them by providing them with monetary support, weapons and training. They gave them their blessings and sent them to Cuba to cause disruption. CIA did not send them alone. They arranged warships and aircraft which preceded and followed the protestors.

As usual, CIA found a few rebels in Cuba. They prepared them by providing them with monetary support, weapons and training. They gave them their blessings and sent them to Cuba to cause disruption. CIA did not send them alone. They arranged warships and aircraft which preceded and followed the protestors. CIA did not trust the local protestors alone and was ready for a huge attack.

The people who operated those warships and aircraft and who were ready to attack Cubans were Americans. But they planned not to reveal their nationality and decided to cover up everything as Cuba's internal revolt.

Their excuse was that local Cubans were protesting against Castro. They would attack Castro's army, and their eventual goal was to send Castro out of the country or end his life. *We are not responsible for the actions of others. Peace!*

As usual, CIA found a few rebels in Cuba. They prepared them by providing them with monetary support, weapons and training. They gave them their blessings and sent them to Cuba to cause disruption. CIA did not send them alone. They arranged warships and aircraft which preceded and followed the protestors.

But America/CIA's dream vanished very soon. Their plan which found success many times, failed miserably in Cuba. The local revolt which CIA was waiting for did not happen at all. The protestors they sent against Fidel Castro were caught by the public and were thrashed. Public dragged them to the police station before they started to speak anything against Castro.

CIA did not bother with what the people of the nation thought. It was difficult for them to overturn governments which was formed with the support of the majority. Cubans had an unimaginable unity that the CIA did not even dream of. They trusted Castro with all their heart. They protested against all who opposed Castro even if it was the Almighty. CIA understood that they could not be divided and conquered like others.

The situation however, went out of control before they realised it. American aircraft which were waiting to barge in and attack when the revolt started were shot and destroyed. Kennedy or CIA could not send additional forces to help them. Since they planned everything in the background, they could not do anything boldly.

The revolt was controlled under Fidel Castro's direct guidance. Most of the protestors sent by the US were killed and the rest were arrested. The Kennedy government was embarrassed. They could not say out aloud what happened and at the same time, they could not hide it too.

The revolt was controlled under Fidel Castro's direct guidance. Most of the protestors sent by the US were killed and the rest were arrested. The Kennedy government was embarrassed. They could not say out aloud what happened and at the same time, they could not hide it too.

Cuba was a tiny country compared to the US. The CIA was embarrassed that they faced failure with Cuba. But they could not do anything in that situation. Their arrogance that they could overpower anybody and anywhere was brought to a halt in Cuba.

The CIA sat down and started to analyse the events that happened. *Who was that Fidel Castro? Wasn't he the one who captured the government through a military revolution? Why are the people attracted towards him?*

Only when they analysed the situation in this angle, they realised the entire dimension of the person that was Castro. The public support which Castro had among the Cubans was not achieved through threats, nor through the frustration that he was better than the others.

Castro gained control of the government overthrowing Fulgencio Batista, a fascist ruler who was ruling Cuba before. Hence, people trusted Castro completely as the person who got them freedom and who could take Cuba to greater heights. In short, Castro's popularity was not due to individual worship but due to the fact that the people were happy with his policies.

The CIA could not understand that. They started again with vengeance—no leader was infallible. They didn't look for protestors then. The CIA spies infiltrated all of Cuba. All of them had the same goal—kill Castro somehow.

We already looked into the brilliant tricks they did at the beginning of this chapter. They could not even touch Castro's shadow until the end. They did not gain wisdom even after several failures. They committed several other immature mistake to decrease the affection Cubans had for Castro.

Some wizard tipped off CIA that Cubans were mesmerised by Castro's magnificent beard. They started making plans on how to remove Castro's beard. CIA tried to sprinkle thallium salt in Castro's shoes. When this chemical mixed in the bloodstream, all his body hair would fall off and the people would lose their fascination for Castro. This 'professional' plan ended in failure. CIA was discouraged and continued to degrade Castro's image among the Cubans.

Some wizard tipped off CIA that Cubans were mesmerised by Castro's magnificent beard. They started making plans on how to remove Castro's beard. CIA tried to sprinkle thallium salt in Castro's shoes. When this chemical mixed in the bloodstream, all his body hair would fall off and the people would lose their fascination for Castro. This 'professional' plan ended in failure. CIA was discouraged and continued to degrade Castro's image among the Cubans.

The next plan was to mix drugs in Castro's cigar when he

was present in a public event. Castro was expected to humiliate himself on smoking the cigar and people were expected to hate him. Control your laughter. There was another mega comedy plan which would shrink all the other plans in comparison.

They took Cuban's religious belief into their plans. They preached that only when an atheist like Castro's government is brought down, would God bless them. Cubans do not believe in anything so easily when compared to others. CIA understood that and arranged for an ostentatious 'incarnation' event.

The incarnation was not of a regular person. It was Jesus's incarnation. Their story, screenplay and dialogues revolved around this plot. Jesus was ready to come back to the earth. But he was hesitant to set foot in Cuba where an atheist was ruling. They arranged grandiose graphic arrangements which would make our Bollywood and Kollywood directors ashamed.

They created a huge simulacrum in Cuba's seashore with the help of an American ship. He was supposed to be Jesus Christ. Fidel Castro was supposed to be the rogue who was stopping Jesus from entering the earth. CIA expected Cubans to believe this ploy and pull Castro by his beard and push him into the ocean crying, "Oh Jesus!"

But the Cubans did not believe this incarnation story. No harm was done to Castro's robust image. CIA faced failure one more time.

In spite of all the failures, the CIA has not dropped their attempts to disrupt Castro's rule in Cuba until today. Cuba and Castro are the only thorn that prick the US until now.

When there are several communist rulers and supporters all over the world, why does the US target only Fidel Castro?

There are two reasons for that. The first is that Cuba is a neighbouring nation to the US. They could not tolerate a communist government at such close proximity. They could not abide with the fact that they were unable to destroy such a tiny country.

The next reason was that Castro was not only a communist supporter but also supported the Soviet Union and that annoyed the US. How could they keep their enemy under their foot and be content?

What was the Soviet Union doing in Cuba? CIA's spying hands extended into Cuba to find the answer to this question.

❑

6
Eyes All Over the World

A Russian approached a CIA agent in Moscow.

"I would like to help you," he said.

There was only a single meaning for the word 'help' in the spying dictionary—'I would like to sell my country's secrets to you, how much will I get?'

The person who volunteered was not a common man. He was an important officer in the Soviet Union military's then intelligence wing named GRU. He himself was volunteering to work as a CIA spy.

In general, CIA should be elated at his offer. It was about to get a spy within the inner circle of the impenetrable Soviet Union government. The CIA could get all the secrets of the Soviets after that. But CIA looked at the officer named Oleg

Penkovskiy with suspicion. It rejected his offer and stepped back.

What happened here? The Soviet Union became a mysterious place in the communist rule. The Soviets closed their border and nobody knew what was happening inside. The American government was struggling to find out their plans.

In those days, if an intelligence agency was performing at the same level as CIA, it was Soviet Union's KGB—Komitet Gosudarstvennoy Bezopasnosti. In fact, KGB officers and spies were superior to CIA in several aspects. The Cold War between the US and the Soviet Union was at its peak then. Both parties wanted to know what the other one was doing.

In such a situation, when a major officer came forward with information, why did CIA refuse to take up the offer?

Why?

In those days, if an intelligence agency was performing at the same level as CIA, it was Soviet Union's KGB—Komitet Gosudarstvennoy Bezopasnosti. In fact, KGB officers and spies were superior to CIA in several aspects. The Cold War between the US and the Soviet Union was at its peak then. Both parties wanted to know what the other one was doing.

So, CIA sent a few of its spies in the disguise of officers to Moscow. Their task was to find out local people who might work as CIA agents. These intelligence agents worked(?) at the American embassy during day and started their actual work in the evening. They participated in the events and parties where the Soviet Union's higher officials and important people visited and watched if anyone of them suited their purpose to work as a spy.

While the CIA was searching for spies in the Soviet Union, KGB penetrated deep into the US. The KGB spies sent all the happenings in the US to Moscow with precision. Moreover, KGB wanted to attack the US. It was aware of the fact that US was searching for local spies in the Soviet Union. So the KGB planned to manipulate the situation to its benefit.

According to their plan, KGB planted its trusted officers and public to act America-friendly. They either met CIA officers directly or circumstantially and criticised the Soviet Union government. On hearing their 'contempt' towards the Soviet government, CIA took them as their spies. They paid each of them well and tried to find out the secrets of the Soviet Union.

But, CIA couldn't get any useful information from these 'spies'. Moreover, they were sending all the activities of CIA to KGB periodically. CIA realised this treachery only after a long time. The situation went from bad to worse soon. CIA was in a deep state of confusion as it did not know who were the real supporters and who were the 'double agents' sent by KGB.

In short, KGB baited CIA and caught them right by the collar. After that incident, the Americans watched all the Russians with suspicion. So, there was no wonder in CIA being sceptical at Oleg Penkovskiy's offer. *What if he too was a KGB spy?*

But at the same time, the CIA could not refrain from spying on the Soviet Union. It was under constant worry about what arrangements and advanced weapons the Soviets might have to attack the US. This worry forced the CIA to find new ways to penetrate the Soviet Union.

During the initial days, the CIA dropped its agents inside the Soviet border through parachutes. Since this was dangerous, it started to send balloons with secret cameras attached to it. The Soviet Union noticed these balloons and dismantled them to analyse their mechanism. They came to know all about CIA's plans through it.

During the initial days, the CIA dropped its agents inside the Soviet border through parachutes. Since this was dangerous, it started to send balloons with secret cameras attached to it. The Soviet Union noticed these balloons and dismantled them to analyse their mechanism.

The Soviet Union called the media immediately. They proved with evidence that the US was secretly spying on them, camouflaging it under the reason of weather research.

The CIA did not have any other tricks in the hat after that. It kept the balloons away and started to think of the next step. CIA had the necessity to know all about the Soviet Union's activities. Even if it failed a little, the Americans might face another attack like Pearl Harbour attack.

The CIA was ready to spend any amount for it. *What is actually happening behind the iron curtain? What is the Russian special military doing? What is the extent of their military strength? How far is their nuclear research? Hearsay is that they have missiles which travel across continents and right now it was directed towards the US. Are these messages true?*

There were questions all around. But no answers for them. The CIA was losing its patience.

On 1 May 1960, an American aircraft of the type 'Lockheed U-2' started from Pakistan and flew towards Norway. The pilot who manoeuvred the craft was Francis Gary Powers. Pakistan and Norway both were not an issue. The Soviet Union which was in between became the trouble. The Soviet Union came to know about the American aircraft which was flying over the border. The Soviet Union immediately decided that it was a spy plane. So it tried to attack and destroy it.

On 1 May 1960, an American aircraft of the type 'Lockheed U-2' started from Pakistan and flew towards Norway. The pilot who manoeuvred the craft was Francis Gary Powers. Pakistan and Norway both were not an issue. The Soviet Union which was in between became the trouble.

The U-2 craft lost its control in the attack and started to go down. Pilot Powers escaped alive by jumping in his parachute. Soviet Union soldiers captured both the pilot and the American aircraft. But they did not reveal this information to the media.

When the US lost its aircraft, would it sit idle? The US announced that one of its research aircraft was missing. The Soviet Union's then President Nikita Khrushchev waited for the announcement and released a report stating that the Soviets had shot down an aircraft which came to spy on them.

The Americans accepted that the fallen aircraft was theirs. But they denied that it was a spy plane and maintained an innocent face. All their secrets were revealed after that. The

Soviet Union released American pilot, Powers, the secret camera which was inside the U-2 craft and the pictures of Soviet Union which were recorded in the camera one by one.

The US started researching about unmanned spy planes and satellites. CIA's major weapon for the next few years was just technological spies. Although it took a major portion of the annual budget, it enabled the CIA to spy on the entire world from its own location.

The US and CIA were embarrassed to the core. It was proven without any doubt that they had spied on the Soviet Union. This affected diplomatic relations between both the nations. Khrushchev demanded an apology from the US for its spying activity. The US President Dwight D Eisenhower downright refused it.

The CIA did not bother about these political pressures. Its worry was how to spy upon the Soviet Union.

If a spy was sent through a parachute, the Soviets would capture him and send him to prison. If the CIA sent a spy balloon, they would burst it. If it sent an aircraft, they would shoot it down. What would the CIA do?

The US decided not to trust anybody and started to use technology. The US started researching about unmanned spy planes and satellites. CIA's major weapon for the next few years was just technological spies. Although it took a major portion of the annual budget, it enabled the CIA to spy on the entire world from its own location.

Once, while the CIA was spying on the world, a news from Cuba jabbed them. Soviet Union ships often travelled to and from Cuba!

If the US asks 'what relation do you have with Soviet Union?' the bearded Fidel Castro would not let out even a word. Khrushchev would be worse than Castro in answering them.

So the CIA decided to find the answer themselves. They sent their 'U-2' spy planes to Cuba. Although Castro's protective force was strong, the Cubans did not have advanced weapons or current technology like the Soviet Union. So, they could not stop the US technological invasion. American aircraft photographed several Cuban places and went back home. The CIA closely analysed these photographs.

The CIA did not require any special vision to find out the new danger that had bloomed in Cuba. The photographs clearly showed that a few missile bases were constructed in Cuba. But, Cuba was a slowly developing nation overcoming economic ban by the US and other issues. How did it obtain the fund to construct missiles?

Cuba didn't have enough funds. But the Soviet Union had it. The US understood that both of their long-term enemies had joined hands and had started acting together. It was one of the Soviet Union's diplomatic moves. It need not manufacture missiles which could travel across the continents. It was enough if the Soviets could create missiles which could travel a shorter distance. Those missiles cannot travel all the way from the Soviet Union and attack the US. But what if they are launched from the neighbouring Cuba?

The Soviet Union might have decided that it was the only way to threaten the US. Fidel Castro welcomed the Soviet Union for its noble cause and allowed the Soviets into his nation.

The US intelligence found that secret spying would not help them any longer and declared that Soviet missiles were getting ready for an attack in Cuba. Their agents did not reveal how they got the information. The American President Kennedy criticised that it was an indirect war against America. The US declared that the happenings in Cuba were against American safety and this would have to be stopped.

The US intelligence found that secret spying would not help them any longer and declared that Soviet missiles were getting ready for an attack in Cuba. Their agents did not reveal how they got the information. The American President Kennedy criticised that it was an indirect war against America.

Would Castro listen? He ignored these comments and continued with his regular duties.

US lost its patience at a stage and declared that it was planning to wage a war against Cuba in October end, 1962. The affair came to an end only after that. The Soviet Union came forward to remove its missiles from Cuba. US agencies also stopped their attack plan consequently.

But even then, USA was not ready to completely trust the Soviet Union or Cuba. CIA sent spy planes over these two countries and continued to take photographs every minute. Through these photographs, it was confirmed that Soviet missiles were being removed from Cuba. Only when the confirmation message reached the US president through a CIA report, he breathed with ease.

If the Soviet Union's missiles were tested successfully in Cuba, they could have destroyed any of the American cities. The fact that they had escaped from such a dire end, made CIA work even harder. The Soviet Union which had set up missiles in Cuba might even threaten the US from some uninhabited island. There was no guarantee that the Soviets would not make such an attempt again.

So the CIA intensified its intelligence activities further. The CIA wanted to be informed of everything anybody did around the world which might support the enemies of the US or were against the US. It did not distinguish between friendly and unfriendly nations. The CIA started to send spy planes to all nations and photographed everything. It created secret CIA offices in many cities and brought in local agents.

The CIA wanted to be informed of everything anybody did around the world which might support the enemies of the US or were against the US. It did not distinguish between friendly and unfriendly nations. The CIA started to send spy planes to all nations and photographed everything. It created secret CIA offices in many cities and brought in local agents.

In the intelligence field, human spies have more respect than the machines. But humans cannot be trusted in all the situations. CIA had the necessity to monitor the world on all days of the year around the clock. From where did the CIA get so many agents?

Technology helped CIA in that aspect. It started to use satellites for its intelligence activities. Manufacturing a satellite and sending it to space was a costly affair. The American government enabled it by increasing CIA's annual budget periodically. Nobody questioned why so many dollars had to be wasted to spy on foreign countries. Even if somebody asked the CIA, it answered them through two words—national security.

Until the late 1970s, the US did not reveal about its spy satellites. Enemies would shoot spies if sent through aircraft. What could they do if satellites were used?

During the peak of the Cold War, the US and the Soviet Union both were using advanced technology to spy on the other nation. Due to this, the CIA's budget and power were increased severalfold. The CIA which was formed to safeguard its own nation was slowly growing into a super power. While its strength increased, its basic goal started changing into something else.

Let me explain this. Assume we have a watchman at our house. We instruct him not to let any outsiders enter our house. For safety purposes, we give him a bamboo cane. The bamboo cane turns into a thick lathi, later into a pistol and then to an AK-47. Cameras are set up all over the house. The watchman's glory increases with a few subordinates. What will he do later? He peeps into the neighbouring house in order to protect own house. He threatens them. If he doesn't like what happens there, he interferes in their house and causes trouble.

Don't you think it is atrocious? CIA's evolution was similar to it.

CIA which was interfering in other countries' affairs right from the beginning, started to function with additional power in the 1970s. The agents had their eyes all over the world with the help of satellites by having spies in almost all the countries, advanced gadgets, and arrangements to eavesdrop on telephonic conversations, letters and other communications.

CIA's primary goal was to find out if anything was being planned against the US. But indirectly, it did everything in its power to make everybody to think like the US, support American policies and if anybody refused to do so, cause trouble for them.

Many say that the reason for the Cold War between the US and the Soviet Union was primarily due to the CIA. We cannot confirm if this news is true or not. But the CIA is to be held responsible for making the US, the 'watchman of the world'.

❑

7
Rowdy

That was an ordinary 'theft case'!

Five people entered an office and tried to steal something. They were caught by a patrolman who came that way. Even the judge who presided over the investigation was not very interested in it. He watched the proceedings with disinterest and was calculating for how long could the accused be granted jail term.

But the public prosecutor was not ready to forgo the investigation so easily. He claimed that the case involved a mystery and couldn't be ignored.

What mystery could a break-in hide?

When the five accused men were questioned, it came to be known that they were Cuban refugees. They did not appear to be thieves who were stealing due to poverty. Each of them had enough money in their pockets.

What was the need for them to steal when they had plenty of cash with them? Even if they decided to rob something, why did they choose to rob the office of a political party? Why did they have unknown electronic devices with them? Why did they give false names when they were caught?

The judge started to take interest in the case. He started to question the accused with suspicion.

The judge started to take interest in the case. He started to question the accused with suspicion. After much persuasion, one among the five talked. "I am a Cuban refugee. I worked as a security consultant for CIA earlier." The case which was an ordinary theft case until then turned into one of the most important cases in the history named as the 'Watergate scandal'.

After much persuasion, one among the five talked. "I am a Cuban refugee. I worked as a security consultant for CIA earlier."

The case which was an ordinary theft case until then turned into one of the most important cases in the history named as the 'Watergate scandal'.

Everybody knew about the dubious activities CIA did in Cuba. Five men who were associated with them, who were Cuban refugees, were doing something suspicious at the party office of the Democratic Party which was a major US opposition party, at midnight.

The Watergate scandal brought out several shocking news to the world. For the first time, Americans started to look at their intelligence agencies with annoyance. What were they actually doing on the pretext of protecting the US? They were causing trouble in foreign nations. They were supporting terrorists by providing them money and weapons.

Moreover, it was election time in the US. President Richard Milhous Nixon was working hard to retain his ruling post. While considering all these points, the American public was able to predict what had happened in the Watergate hotel campus during that night.

When the Americans realised that their intelligence agency not only spied on others, but also spied on their own people, they were shocked. They could not accept this treachery.

The person who was affected the most due to the Watergate scandal was President Nixon. He was forced to resign his post in an embarrassing way. But Americans were not satisfied with that. Nixon was a politician, and nothing better could be expected from him. What happened to the intelligence agencies?

The US had FBI to handle internal affairs and CIA to handle international affairs. Although their boundaries were mutually exclusive, the authority contest among both of them couldn't be avoided. They worked together in spying on the Americans. They employed several methods to achieve it. A few of them were against humanity and illegal too.

The Watergate scandal brought out several shocking news to the world. For the first time, Americans started to look at their intelligence agencies with annoyance. *What were they actually doing on the pretext of protecting the US? They were causing trouble in foreign nations. They were supporting terrorists by providing them money and weapons. They were overturning governments which opposed them. Or they were killing the leaders of those governments. Were they right?*

If somebody asked these questions to the CIA, it would have laughed at their faces. But now, the questions were asked by the Americans themselves. The CIA was being funded by tax money, so it had the responsibility of answering their questions.

There was nothing right in its actions. So the CIA remained silent. Its partner FBI too remained the same. Even if they had broken their silence, what could they have said? They might have said that all was done for 'national security,' but no one was ready to believe the same excuse again.

Following the Watergate scandal, the focus light fell upon the activities of the CIA. People started to monitor what was happening, with sharp eyes. Magazines started to criticise its action for the first time.

While CIA was thinking about how to recover its image, one official thought out of the box.

His name was William E Colby. He was the vice president of CIA's action department. He said that it was time for CIA to do some self-introspection.

He said, "There is no use in emotionalising the issue. There has been a mistake. If not, so many people would not have turned against us. So, let us think about it and if we have any fault, let us try to rectify it."

If he had said the same in some other situation, CIA would have handed him his dismissal order and sent him out. But at that time, it realised that there was some truth in his speech.

SO, CIA director, James R Schlesinger accepted Colby's idea. He brought in his senior officers and discussed with them in detail.

"Friends, we might have made a few mistakes in the hurry of safeguarding our country. Or we might have heard about the wrongdoings of others. We have conducted all our activities in secret. Now, outsiders have found about all our mistakes and have embarrassed us. However, we have to spy on others. If somebody else spies upon us, it is a shame to us. So, it is essential that we reach a decision in this issue.

"The CIA was formed for specific reasons. The constitution has laid a few rules based on which we have to act. But, are we following them in reality? Or are we acting according to our own wish? Where and when have we compromised on the basic goal of the CIA? Crossed the legal line?

"The CIA was formed for specific reasons. The constitution has laid a few rules based on which we have to act. But, are we following them in reality? Or are we acting according to our own wish? Where and when have we compromised on the basic goal of the CIA? Crossed the legal line? We have to note down everything and record them. There is no need to feel ashamed or scared in this issue. Only if we know our mistakes, we can rectify them."

When the CIA director said so, other officers started to open up. They made a detailed list about what they felt was wrong in CIA operations and the methods they used. When these complaints given by the CIA agents were compiled, it crossed seven hundred pages. Colby named this secret document as 'Family Jewels'.

The American government was more shocked than surprised on looking at Colby's list. The reason was that most of the listed-out incidents took place with their approval and blessing. If the information was leaked out, they would face major heat.

The former CIA director resigned during this time. William Colby was selected as the new director. The first crisis he faced after taking charge was to decide what to do with the Family Jewels. Even Colby did not expect so many problems, complaints and violations because of the CIA actions. He read the list completely and was overwhelmed at the extent of the atrocities committed.

But, even then he did not consider the encyclopedia-sized complaint record as a negative thing. CIA was acting upon its own for so long and he considered that the self-analysis was necessary for the organisation. If CIA activities improve after that, it would be beneficial only to them.

So, William Colby took the 'Family Jewels' record and went to the American government. "Sir/Madam, we have listed out all the problems inside the CIA. Please read it and do the needful."

The American government was more shocked than surprised on looking at Colby's list. The reason was that most of the listed-out incidents took place with their approval and blessing. If the information was leaked out, they would face major heat.

Moreover, if they acted against the CIA for those actions, how could the US safeguard the world*? Is spying an easy task? How can anybody condemn a few violations?* After a long consideration, the US decided not to act on the issue. They just ignored Colby and his list.

But the news leaked out. Seymour Hersh from *New York Times* sniffed out the matter.

He directly questioned Colby. "Is it true that the CIA has made such a list?" Colby tried to give a negative response to his question and that created a huge scandal.

A detailed article was published in the 22 December 1974 issue of the *New York Times*. Several issues including CIA foreign affairs and spying on American citizens were censured. The CIA image was already tarnished in the Watergate scandal. This news added fuel to the fire.

An investigation committee was formed under the leadership of Senate member Frank Church. It was named as 'Church Committee' and they investigated the activities of the American intelligence agencies and their violations in detail. The Church Committee gave their conclusions in a series of reports. The misconduct of American intelligence agents and the recommendations to right them were debated in detail in the reports.

During these Church Committee investigations which took place in mid-1970s, CIA's attempts in killing foreign leaders came to light. Many were shocked and couldn't find out the reason for why an intelligence agency which was created for gathering information would try to murder others. When they came to know about the methods it employed for its killing missions, the shock turned into contempt.

Apart from the CIA, the US too was ashamed due to this. Even Americans wanted them to stop such activities. So, a special order was issued by the American government. All the attempts against foreign leaders were banned through this order.

The issue did not stop here. CIA spying upon Americans was proved without any doubt. It had made several violations including reading others' letters, following innocent Americans and recording information about them and many others.

When the CIA was asked about the need for such actions, it replied that it suspected them to be foreign spies and hence did the surveillance. But the Church Committee clearly mentioned that it was wrong of the CIA to have done such an immoral act. Several violations were known to be done by the CIA outside the US too.

When the CIA was asked about the need for such actions, it replied that it suspected them to be foreign spies and hence did the surveillance. But the Church Committee clearly mentioned that it was wrong of the CIA to have done such an immoral act.

Several violations were known to be done by the CIA outside the US too. Their agents injected drugs into the criminals or those who were suspected to be criminals to bring out the truth from them. They hid and tortured several people without letting the world know that they were arrested for a crime. They had even used the help of the Mafia for a few activities. Their offence list was a long one.

The Church Committee described CIA as a 'wild elephant' which had gone out of control. It recommended to decrease its power and not to allow it to act independently. The reports of the secretly held Church Committee and most of the 'Family Jewels' documents have been revealed to the public now. Just during that period, Americans also learnt that CIA's power has been controlled.

Several of the CIA intelligence activities were restricted by the Church Committee. Or they were changed. The committee declared clearly it was not necessary for such intense intelligence work and spying on others' affairs. It was especially mentioned that the CIA was not to interfere in fellow Americans' personal lives any more.

Reigning in a wild horse like CIA which was acting on its own will was a shock. But, while looking at it closely, we can understand that it would have surely happened sometime in the future if not then. Several of the CIA officers were offended by it. "We do not claim to be innocent. We made a few mistakes, but we did them with the approval of the government," they said.

They claimed that an intelligence agency could be run without any of their actions. *National security is a serious issue. There should be no compromise in it. There is no use in coddling the criminals, they have to be treated with iron hands.* Those officers were worried that the trust and the rights the government gave to the CIA, to know about American enemies, had been revoked.

Another concern was that several of the violations found by the Church Committee had happened seven or eight years ago. CIA itself had found them to be wrong and had rectified them. Its major apprehension was that it was not fair to rekindle old fires and to embarrass the CIA. The 'rowdy' title given to the CIA humiliated it.

The American government did not mind the unease of the CIA. It concentrated only on controlling the intelligence agency just for the sake of appeasing the public.

Starting from the end of the 1970s, CIA's power was reduced gradually. The huge budget which was given to them was considerably decreased. Several agents were let go. The activities of the remaining agents were monitored with high scrutiny.

Many were pleased on the CIA being constrained. But some warned them. "This is not necessary. Who will take the responsibility if something similar to the Pearl Harbour attack takes place in the future?"

Their warning proved to be true at the end. Within twenty years of restricting the CIA, several powerful enemies emerged against the US. They were ready to attack the US.

Several of them were reared by America themselves, especially CIA!

❑

8
Secret, Top Secret!

The image that conjures in our mind upon hearing the term 'intelligence agency' is entirely different from the reality.

Agents in disguise, several gadgets in their hands and bags, guns in holsters, sharp-eyed agents following somebody in the dark or rain, fixing bugs in hidden areas known only to cockroaches, photocopying secret documents and sending signals through wireless radios.

CIA too has all these, but their real action starts only after that.

When the CIA was formed in 1947, it was not a huge network. It started to operate in a small rented building in Washington just like other government agencies. Only when the world wars ended, they were able to shift to a bigger office.

Even then, there was a compulsion that their office had to be adjacent to the White House.

When Kennedy became the president, a small change was made to this practice. He did not like to distribute the 'National Intelligence Daily' to everybody. What is the respect for the president's post if everybody knows about every secret? Only when there are secrets known only to him, there will be a reverence towards him.

The reason was that the American president was the major 'customer' of CIA. Their primary task was to gather information for him. The information included everything right from the rain in Islamabad, severe dust storm in New Delhi, processions in Jordan, to the social changes happening in other nations, military actions and scientific advancements.

During CIA's initial days, this report was called the 'National Intelligence Daily'. This daily report was given to almost 250 senior officials who were prominent members in the American government. It was similar to a newspaper, but a top secret newspaper. The information present in it would not have been known to anybody but the CIA.

When Kennedy became the president, a small change was made to this practice. He did not like to distribute the 'National Intelligence Daily' to everybody. What is the respect for the president's post if everybody knows about every secret? Only when there are secrets known only to him, there will be a reverence towards him.

Kennedy ordered the CIA to provide a daily report to him alone. The report was a short one which had information that the president wanted to know. It was named as the President's

Daily Brief (PDB). The 8–10 page PDB was the most secret document in the US. A separate team was formed in CIA just to create and give the report to the president.

The reason was that George Bush operated as the director of CIA before entering politics. So he was aware of how to utilise the intelligence department to their best. Bush asked the CIA officers who prepared and sent the PDB report, to read it to him.

The American president's first job every morning was to browse the PDB. Even if he was out of station, the PDB had to be sent to him through secured fax. The PDB which was sent only to the US president was sent to a few other important officials later. The president determined who could read the report.

The president took many military decisions based on the report which was called the 'book'. So, it was the CIA's responsibility to include all the last-minute information the report.

So, the PDB report which was prepared in the night would be compiled again in the morning including all the information which came in through the night. New information, pictures and discussions would be added and then sent to print.

When George Bush took charge as the US president in 1989, the importance of the PDB increased. The reason was that George Bush operated as the director of CIA before entering politics. So he was aware of how to utilise the intelligence department to their best. Bush asked the CIA officers who prepared and sent the PDB report, to read it to him.

It was not enough to just prepare the report, the background information about the events mentioned and additional details had to be explained to him. The doubts raised by the president had to be clarified immediately.

The president might ask for additional information while reading the PDB. If the CIA didn't have the information asked by him, they had to gather it somehow within the next day and include it in the next day's PDB. If not, the officer concerned had to face ill consequences.

Sometimes, based on the importance of the question asked, information might have to be gathered immediately. So, the practice of having the CIA office next to the president's residence became the norm.

Not only the information present in PDB, but also the source of the information was also kept top secret. When the news about the source leaks out, it might cause danger to the person involved, so CIA need not reveal the information according to the law.

The CIA office operates from more than hundred countries across the world, not only in the enemy nations but in the friendly nations too. The reason is that, just like politics, there is no enemy or friend forever. A popular example for this is that Iraq which had US support during the Iran–Iraq war, turned against the US later.

So, the US continues its intelligence activities in friendly nations as well as enemy nations. They do not leave the neutral nations too.

CIA calls its offices 'stations'. We might not even have heard of the names of many nations where CIA has its station.

According to the law, the CIA should not gather information within the country. Even if they have to interrogate a US citizen for some cause, there should be no hidden questions. They have to introduce themselves as CIA and ask the questions directly. They should not spy on them without their knowledge.

But the US requires to keep tabs on the happenings of those countries too.

The offices do not have neon lights flashing with the name 'CIA'. Most of the countries have just a single or two member offices. In some countries, a complete network of 20–30 agents is also available. An officer will be in charge of the team. He is known as Chief of Station (COS). He is responsible for collecting all the details related to the country.

COS assigns a few officers for the task. In smaller countries, he himself might be needed to get into the field. These officers are the agents who help the US. They find suitable spies according to their mission. The COS is responsible for verifying the information collected by the agents and sending it to the head office.

CIA's important network mostly include foreign stations. But, at times, they have work inside the country too.

According to the law, the CIA should not gather information within the country. Even if they have to interrogate a US citizen for some cause, there should be no hidden questions. They have to introduce themselves as CIA and ask the questions directly. They should not spy on them without their knowledge.

But the case was different with politicians, scientists and officers who visit the US from foreign countries. CIA had used them for their benefit and had spied on the foreign countries.

CIA is still continuing its hunt for people who will work along with them. They include themselves in the conferences and parties where foreigners participate in huge numbers. Sometimes, they themselves arrange for visas and find people for their cause.

A huge amount is allotted for this cause in the CIA's annual budget. Good pay and benefits will be awarded to those who come forward with information that favours the US. The information about them will be safeguarded as well.

They cannot post an advertisement in the newspaper—'Wanted, reliable spies!' They have to search the network through a magnifying lens.

If Americans visit a major country for business or pleasure and return home, a CIA officer will meet them immediately. The officer will ask for everything they saw and people whom they met in the foreign country and note it down carefully.

But that is not enough for the CIA. They have to know what happens inside the foreign embassy in their country and the information transferred between their country and the embassy. So they look for spies within the country.

CIA's first bait are the foreigners who visit their country. Who like the American life among them? Who are addicted to its luxuries?

American life is fun-filled. But, a lot of money is required to enjoy all that it offers. CIA's first target are the foreigners who sigh with a longing for those luxuries. The next target are those who do not align with the policies of their rulers in each country. CIA smooth talk them and bring them into their circle.

CIA is still continuing its hunt for people who will work along with them. They include themselves in the conferences and parties where foreigners participate in huge numbers. Sometimes, they themselves arrange for visas and find people for their cause.

CIA has used blackmail on rare occasions. Most of its officers say that threatening a person to act according to their wish do not work out in most of the cases. They do not hand over the appointment order to the person whom they have selected as the 'future spy'. They wait for several weeks and months and monitor their activities.

Who is the person? What does he do for living? What is his hobby? What are his family/personal problems? What are his urgent needs? What should be done to attract him?

If the person under scrutiny likes music, the CIA agent who follows him should learn at least the basics of music. If he likes fishing, the agent has to wait with a fishing rod for hours along with him.

Only after establishing a regular contact with him, they talk to the individual in person. They start with harmless social questions and then come to their agenda. *Are you in need of money? We are ready to shower you in dollars. Do you want to settle down here? Immigration is waiting for you. Are you sick?*

We will arrange for the latest treatment. Did you do anything wrong? No problem, let us erase your past.

CIA officers are expert in finding what a person wants and lure him with their own needs. Is there a human alive without any weaknesses? They find out that weakness and utilise it.

Many of those chosen by the CIA will come forward to work with them willingly. But a few of them refuse to betray their own country. CIA does not bother with those rejections. If they are to be ashamed by such rejections, they cannot run an intelligence agency.

The CIA has a procedure to test the foreign spies. They ask questions for which they already know the answer initially. Based on the answer given by the person, they allot tasks to him. When they start to trust a spy after the test, a CIA officer will be assigned to that person. After that, all the information gathered by the spy will reach the headquarters only through that particular officer.

All the spies who come forward to work with CIA have a monthly salary. In addition to that, bonuses will be paid to them whenever they give information to their CIA officer. The salary and bonus is not a fixed amount. It depends upon the qualification of the spy/his current status/the importance of the information given and many other factors.

The CIA has a procedure to test the foreign spies. They ask questions for which they already know the answer initially. Based on the answer given by the person, they allot tasks to him. When they start to trust a spy after the test, a CIA officer will be assigned to that person. After that, all the information gathered by the spy will reach the headquarters only through that particular officer.

Even after such a careful planning, CIA officers or agents might get caught by the local police or the intelligence officers. During such situations, the situation has to be handled with much care. The Americans who were under the cover of embassy employees escape easily from such crises.

CIA had rented several individual houses in each of their operating nations solely for the purpose of the discussion between the spies and their officers. All of their conversations were recorded without their knowledge. This may sound interesting while reading it as a story. But sitting in a foreign nation and spying on them is not an easy task. If they get caught, their lives might end.

So, the CIA arranges a 'Colgate' security ring for those officers who work in foreign countries. Most of them will work for the US embassy in that country. Some might have been given a new name and a non-threatening identity too. The officers hide behind this false identity and involve themselves in the secret missions. They have to find a convincing cover story for each time they travel to meet their local spies. Even if they get caught, they should be ready with a credible reason for their presence in the location.

Even after such a careful planning, CIA officers or agents might get caught by the local police or the intelligence officers. During such situations, the situation has to be handled with much care. The Americans who were under the cover of embassy employees escape easily from such crises. In some situations, exchanges might be made to release them. Spies who were caught in the US will be released instead of them in such cases.

While compared to these officers, local spies known as 'agents' face higher danger. If they get caught in gathering secret information, the US will not help them and at the same time they do not get local support too.

Although there are many perils involved, several still volunteer themselves to work as a spy in almost all the countries. The major reason for that is the money they offer for their services.

CIA maintains the information about its spies as top secret. Each agent is given a code number/name at the beginning. After that, their real name will not be used in any of the CIA documents. Everything will be mentioned using secret codes. The real name associated with the secret code will be kept as a secret. Nobody can get this information with ease. It will be hidden well like a demon's life.

The CIA has selected numerous secret agents in each country. A marvellous network has also been constructed to collect and compile the information given by them. The information collected in each country reaches the local CIA station. They are responsible of compiling them and sending them to the head office.

But not all information received can be sent to the head office. They have to be analysed to segregate the important ones from the trivial ones. The CIA officers segregate all the information sent to the head office into four categories based on their importance—Flash, Immediate, Priority and Routine.

Flash and Immediate among these are very important information. The others are less important. But they cannot be ignored. All the petty information has to be sent to the head office without fail. CIA's head office receives information report from all over the world. The officers in charge collect the information and mark them. This is a useful information, so 20 marks. This is not that good, so 3 marks is enough. This is useless, so zero marks. Each information is marked accordingly.

The scores given to the stations are calculated annually and the efficiency of each station is determined. The most important information (the ones which score higher) from each day's report are added to the PDB which is sent to the president.

The CIA's official powers ends with it. The action to be taken based on the information lies in the hands of the president and the Senate. There is some information which they failed to find in the history of the CIA. At the same time, there are instances in which the CIA have found the threat but president and other officers failed to recognise it.

Thus, the US government cannot desert the CIA altogether. At the same time, they fear that it might harm them if more power is given to the CIA. Meanwhile, the CIA has been growing in power for the last five decades.

❑

9
New Alliance

It was the period when the Bolshevik revolution ended and the Soviet Union was formed in Russia.

The task of designing the flag for the new federation was given to an artist. He designed a blood-red flag with a sword at the centre of it. When Lenin saw the flag, he ordered the removal of the sword from the design.

Why should it be removed? Isn't a sword a symbol of bravery?

"That is why it has to be removed," said Lenin. "A sword is needed for those who captures other nations, we oppose it."

The Soviet Union was formed based on such a noble policy. They were adamant in not encroaching on others' lands. But, after half a century, it became a necessity for them to wage war against another country. The Afghanistan war lasted for about ten years. In this war, the Soviet Union lost more than what it gained.

Even after such a careful planning, CIA officers or agents might get caught by the local police or the intelligence officers. During such situations, the situation has to be handled with much care. The Americans who were under the cover of embassy employees escape easily from such crises.

Can the US refrain itself from participating in it? They used the CIA as their representatives to muddle the Afghan pond further.

Before looking into it, it is important to know about the background of the the Soviet Union entering Afghanistan. Afghanistan is a Muslim country. The Soviet Union is a communist federation. Although they are close geographically, they are miles apart in language, culture and several other parameters.

In such situations, the people who live on the border of the countries are the ones who are affected most. The Muslims who were living on the Afghan border of the Soviet Union did not like certain principles of communism. They felt that they were neglected just because they were minorities. Moreover, they strongly believed that communists are against God. They had a few qualms in living under the rule of atheists.

The Soviet Union understood this attitude and provided several political and economic benefits to Afghanistan. A left-wing party was formed in Afghan with the help of the Soviet Union. Everything started well in that party named the People's Democratic Party of Afghanistan (PDPA). But, several commotions including internal politics and rivalry started in 1967.

The US might not even have been aware of the presence of a nation named Afghanistan until then. But when they came to know that the Soviet Union had invaded Afghanistan, they started to prepare themselves to interfere.

Everybody in the party considered themselves to be the future prime ministers. They started bickering among themselves, "Why is he holding the post? Why don't I overturn him and take the post? You are corrupt!" The Afghan political arena started to stink.

In 1973, Daoud overturned the previous government and took charge. A military revolution happened five years later and a small revolution followed it shortly. The situation had started to go out of control.

The Soviet Union did not want to interfere in the Afghan affairs directly. But they wanted the Afghan government to be in their favour. The Afghan political stage was unstable and the new government was taking charge frequently. How could the Soviet Union expect everybody to favour them?

Problems started. A military revolutionary named Hafizullah Amin decided not to support the Soviet Union. The Soviet Union was irritated and sent its army to Afghanistan. The army's mission was not to conquer Afghan and add them to the Soviet Union, but to form a red government within Afghanistan.

The US might not even have been aware of the presence of a nation named Afghanistan until then. But when they came to know that the Soviet Union had invaded Afghanistan, they started to prepare themselves to interfere.

If it was during the world war, the US might have used the pretext that they were helping to defend the Afghans against the Soviet Union. But it was peacetime then, so they had to act indirectly. It had to be an indirect approach and that too in a foreign nation. So, then US President Jimmy Carter called the CIA.

"What is happening in Afghanistan? What can we do in it? The most important question is what will be the immediate and long-term benefits for us?"

When the CIA was formed, it was given a list of rules. Over the period, the CIA had formulated a few rules for themselves. But the right to wage war against a country is not included in both the lists.

However, they could do anything behind the screen. Although they could not march to Afghanistan with army tanks and warcraft holding the US flag, they could oppose the Soviet Union in other ways.

When compared to the huge Soviet Union, Afghanistan was a tiny nation. But, even so, they did not welcome the Soviet Union's presence. The CIA predicted that there would be local opposition for the Soviet invasion in Afghan. As usual, CIA decided to support the opposing group. Their basic goal was to harm the Soviet Union using the protestors.

Afghanistan was an economically backward nation and its revolutionary groups were also impoverished. Although they had enough people in their army, they were a few centuries behind in weaponry. They were not aware of smart war techniques.

This shortcoming was noted by another group even before CIA —Pakistan's intelligence group ISI (Inter-Services Intelligence).

Pakistan's interest in Afghanistan constitutes a separate story. Let us ignore it for now. ISI decided to help the Afghan mujahideens who were fighting against the invasion by the Soviet Union. Their help extended from supplying them with enough food until weapon training and war training began. Pakistan and Afghanistan's borders were opened for this purpose.

Pakistan was responsible for distributing the weapons to several militant groups which were operating in Afghanistan. CIA made a smart calculation in that too. They found out terrorists among the Afghan militant groups who do not have any fear and supplied them with more weapons. They calculated that the Soviet Union would be more affected by it.

CIA was excited about this information. They joined hands with ISI and started to murk the pond. CIA purchased weapons worth 15 million dollars from many countries like China and Egypt to supply them to Afghan militants. These weapons were sent to Pakistan through American aircraft.

Pakistan was responsible for distributing the weapons to several militant groups which were operating in Afghanistan. CIA made a smart calculation in that too. They found out terrorists among the Afghan militant groups who do not have any fear and supplied them with more weapons. They calculated that the Soviet Union would be more affected by it.

Several supports ranging from guns, explosives, electronic gadgets, missiles and chemical weapons were sent from US to Pakistan and finally to Afghanistan. The weight of these materials sent per year was several thousand tons! US did not stop with sending just weapons. Many of the CIA officers purchased season tickets to Pakistan. Many US faces were seen in the ISI offices more than the local faces.

The CIA officers were given two responsibilities. Teaching basic training and advanced technological tips to the ISI officers, agents and spies was the first responsibility. The second one was to provide support and training to the Afghan militants directly.

When Pakistan realised that they had the complete support and blessings of the US, their strength increased. The speed with which the weapons were sent to the militants and war training increased with it.

When the Soviet Union started its Afghan invasion in 1979, they expected to complete their mission within no time as Afghanistan was a small country. But they had to face two strong enemies—ISI and CIA in Afghanistan.

If they had fought in a direct combat, the situation would have been favourable to the Soviet Union. But they hid behind the Afghan militants and prepared them. Moreover, several Muslim youths (popular example: Osama Bin Laden) reached Afghanistan to help the nation.

Afghanistan's terrain consists of forests and mountains which are not easy terrain to be scaled by those unfamiliar with it. The Soviet Union was crippled, not knowing who was attacking them and from where.

CIA looked at everything with a mysterious smile on their face. They could not control their pleasure in having dealt a severe blow to the Soviet Union at the peak of the Cold War.

The war which was supposed to be completed within a short duration, extended to many years due to the behind-the-screen activities. The Afghan militants who received support from ISI and CIA put up a tough fight against the Soviet Union. Although the Soviet Union had brought in additional force and weapons, the war was never-ending.

The war which was supposed to be completed within a short duration, extended to many years due to the behind-the-screen activities. The Afghan militants who received support from ISI and CIA put up a tough fight against the Soviet Union. Although the Soviet Union had brought in additional force and weapons, the war was never-ending.

According to the CIA, it was just a way to weaken the Soviet Union. They had experienced how a nation would lose its strength if it is involved in continuous war, through the Vietnam war. So they wanted to cause severe damage to the Soviet Union using the same technique. Thousands of Soviet Union warriors lost their lives at the hands of Afghan militants. The Soviet Union could not manage the huge expense of such a long war.

The Soviet Union–Afghanistan war which lasted for ten years (1979–89) killed lakhs of people. The count of people who were left destitute also crossed several lakhs. Moreover, the many landmines which were installed during the war are not yet removed completely. Even today, many innocents step on it and lose their lives.

Although the Soviet Union caused severe damage in Afghanistan, they could not completely conquer them. Afghan militants have dealt with them through both direct attack and through guerilla war.

Soviet Union evacuated Afghanistan in the year 1989. ISI–CIA alliance was the one responsible for this and they were overjoyed by it more than the Afghan militants. That was their highest victory until today without any doubts. The victory in Afghanistan has a special place in the history of both ISI and CIA.

The CIA has played and hunted in several nations both before and after Afghanistan. But they caused severe damage to the Soviet Union in the Afghan war. This was a special victory for them. They had to spend several billion dollars to achieve the victory. But even then, the enemy had lost an eye and they remain unaffected, so it was worth their celebration.

The US had several gains in acting behind the Afghanistan war; their loss was less.

But, one incident which occurred as the side effect of the invasion, changed the world's history. That incident became a threat to the existence of CIA, indirectly.

❑

10
Downfall

How far is the gap between the Soviet Union and the US?

This was the single question which hard-pressed two generations of American rulers, military and the intelligence officers. They could not eat or sleep well until they found the answer to the question. Even in their sleep, Soviet comrades invaded their dreams with a multitude of weapons.

The gap was not measured in kilometres, but by several others like bomb gap, missile gap and others just to burden the US.

We are familiar with generation gap, but what is a bomb gap?

Bomb gap was the difference in the bomb making technology between the Soviet Union and the US. Similarly, the difference in missile making technology was called 'missile gap.'

After the Second World War, the Soviet Union hid behind a curtain and nobody knew what was happening in that country. The CIA was also included in the term, 'nobody'. Not only the CIA, no other skilled spy was able to enter into the Soviet Union at that period. So, tensions increased inside the US. They were anxious in not knowing anything about the country..

For example, it was believed that the US was two years ahead of the Soviet Union in nuclear bomb research. At the same time, the US believed that they were behind the Soviet Union by several months in chemical weapons, missiles, satellites and electronic bugs.

The CIA fuelled this belief of the US. Although it is boring to repeat it again, this has to be reminded once again. After the Second World War, the Soviet Union hid behind a curtain and nobody knew what was happening in that country. The CIA was also included in the term, 'nobody'. Not only the CIA, no other skilled spy was able to enter into the Soviet Union at that period.

So, tensions increased inside the US. They were anxious in not knowing anything about the country. *What is happening inside the Soviet Union? Can it be growth or downfall? Or is it another revolution? Are the people progressing or regressing? Are they getting basic amenities inside? Is there any scientific advancement? How big is their military force? What about their weapons?*

But why does the US need such petty information?

A country's political or military strength is primarily based on its growth. Only if the US was aware of the trade growth inside the Soviet Union, the average income of its people, the source of income for the government, the way they spend it and the amount allotted to its military, it could act based the information.

Everything was just happening for the best. If the Soviet Union was found to spend ten dollars for nuclear research, the US was ready to spend twenty dollars for the same. But if they were not aware of the basic information, they could not do anything. They would be uncertain about how much to spend for their nuclear research. They may not know whether twenty dollars was enough or if two hundred or two thousand was needed.

The basis for all the problems endured by the US during the Cold War period was this uncertainty. They were restless always in not knowing what was happening inside the Soviet Union.

The nuclear research, missile design programmes and space research of the Soviet Union was almost at the same level as the US in that period. If the gap was to be measured, there was not much of it. But, since the US did not know about it, they imagined to a great extent and were terrified.

Moreover, several rumours were floating among the Americans. 'Soviet Union has prepared multi-coloured missiles which fly over continents just for the purpose of destroying the US, they are packing heavy chemical weapons to be filled inside the missiles. In addition to that, nuclear bombs which are four times powerful than the ones the US dropped on Japan are being made and they are painting it communist red.'

The problem was that the US did not have anybody to tell them strongly that Soviet Union does not have such powerful weapons or to give them hope. Their imagination was so vivid that they expected the officers of the Soviet Union to sit inside the tall towers of Moscow, nibbling at their sandwiches and ready to demolish the US with the press of a single button.

Frustrated, the US government, increased CIA's budget. CIA were given orders that they should give a 'live' telecast of what was happening inside Russia like a cricket match. It was a tough task to penetrate into the Soviet border and their political and military circles. But CIA continued its efforts without losing hope.

Frustrated, the US government, increased CIA's budget. CIA were given orders that they should give a 'live' telecast of what was happening inside Russia like a cricket match. It was a tough task to penetrate into the Soviet border and their political and military circles. But CIA continued its efforts without losing hope.

In response, KGB—the Soviet Union's intelligence agency played with them. The Cold War was intensified due to the competition between the two intelligence groups.

CIA wanted to get information then—Did the Soviet Union have missiles which were capable of flying over continents? If yes, would they fly to the US?

The questions might look easy, but in spite of all their efforts, they could not find a clear answer to them. The information which they gathered after severe efforts could not be confirmed to be true or false.

The CIA which was used to perform successfully in all the other nations, struggled in gathering even basic information inside the Soviet Union. But they could not admit to this. Won't others look down upon them if they replied that they couldn't find any information?

The Soviet Union's leaders were clever in that aspect. Although they had numerous internal conflicts, they wanted to be considered as an equal opponent by the US. To achieve this, they hid all the information about their economy, trade growth, military and security measures. Or they used double agents and leaked out fake information to the CIA and misled them.

CIA's situation was in distress due to the Soviet's play. If American leaders asked them if Soviet Union had any damage-causing weapons, they blinked without any answers.

Ok, let us leave it. How is the growth of the Soviet Union? Is it raining there? Are people content with their life or are they planning on how to attack the US? Or are they struggling with internal problems? Is the Soviet Union's economy growing or falling?

CIA did not have an answer to any of their questions. The CIA which was used to perform successfully in all the other nations, struggled in gathering even basic information inside the Soviet Union. But they could not admit to this. Won't others look down upon them if they replied that they couldn't find any information?

So, the CIA started to add their own imagination to the little information gathered about the Soviet Union. They started to add more to every count they had. Thus, the US had a false image about the Soviet Union's military and weaponry strength. They believed that the Soviet's strength was several times more than their own and started to spend more for their protection and for weapon and space researches.

It was the biggest downfall in the history of the CIA. The Soviet Union was the only major enemy of the US at that period. While Americans were shivering about what the Soviet Union would do, they were actually sinking down without the strength to oppose anybody. CIA failed to know about it.

While the US was anxious about the Soviet Union's growth, what was really happening inside the Soviet Union?

The secret which was not known to the CIA, came out to the world very late—the Soviet Union was struggling due to severe economic depression.

The reason for Soviet Union's downfall is not relevant to this book. How could CIA fail to know the downfall of such an important nation?

It was the biggest downfall in the history of the CIA. The Soviet Union was the only major enemy of the US at that period. While Americans were shivering about what the

Soviet Union would do, they were actually sinking down without the strength to oppose anybody. CIA failed to know about it.

So, the US fear about the Soviet Union did not falter till the end. CIA, which should have gathered the real status and allayed fears, failed miserably. Reporting an increased military and weaponry force can be forgiven, but failing to notice their economic depression turned out to be a huge mistake. CIA was reporting to the US that the Soviet's growth ratio was good until the end.

If the US had known about the Soviet Union's economic depression, they would have taken some controlling measures on the Soviet Union. The US might have caused the Soviet to shatter earlier. But that did not happen due to CIA's lack of information. The Soviet Union shattered into many countries on its own.

The enemy federation which was a huge challenge to the US for so many years has vanished now. The US, which should have celebrated it, faced the situation with shock. The whole reason for that unbelief was CIA's faulty vision. The Soviet's sudden downfall was a huge shock to the CIA which was giving reports like 'The Soviet Union is flourishing. There is no wonder if they attack us the coming Tuesday'.

Before they recovered from that shock, there came the next thunderstorm. Americans started to ask, 'Since the Soviet Union itself is no more, what is the use of CIA now'? Several requests were made to stop utilising people's tax money on CIA and to close them altogether.

Most of the Americans felt that the CIA was not needed any longer. But the reality is that those who asked for CIA to close down did not understand the actions of CIA completely. CIA started to gain strength at the time when the Cold War started between the Soviet Union and the US. But they did not consider spying on the Soviet Union as their sole responsibility.

The Soviet Union was one among the many targets of CIA. Even when the Cold War was at its peak, they did not spend more than twenty percent of their allocated fund in spying on the Soviet Union. So, the American government considered that CIA could not be dismantled just because the Soviet Union had gone down. They still had several important responsibilities.

The Soviet Union was one among the many targets of CIA. Even when the Cold War was at its peak, they did not spend more than twenty percent of their allocated fund in spying on the Soviet Union. So, the American government considered that CIA could not be dismantled just because the Soviet Union had gone down. They still had several important responsibilities.

But the respect they lost with the public did not return. Since the Soviet threat was no longer there, many started to criticise the CIA. In such a situation, patriotism and national security were not enough reasons for the CIA. Many started to ask what threat did the US have then.

CIA's past mistakes and shortcomings were listed in magazines and media. Voices got strengthened directly and indirectly to stop expenditure on them. The American government could not manage such aversions beyond a certain limit. CIA's power was reduced (again). The budget allocated to them was also reduced considerably.

CIA had never faced such a tough situation before that. Five directors were changed within the next seven years. Nobody could control the situation. In that period, there were a few who supported the CIA. But, the count of people who supported having an intelligence agency for the nation were less than those who argued that it was necessary to control the CIA.

Without any other option, CIA started to minimise its border and acted within that. They were performing the important tasks alone unlike before. But even then, they did not lose hope. They believed that people would realise the importance of intelligence someday.

Ten years later, during the 9/11 attack, CIA's importance increased in the US. Americans realised that intelligence activities are important for a country and gave the required importance to them. But, until then, CIA was made to live as an uninvited guest in the US.

CIA took several actions to improve their image among the public. They released their old secret documents to the public. They tried to maintain a smooth relationship with media and news people. But the severe blow which they received during the Soviet's downfall could not be cured by such small treatments. CIA could not be strengthened as before.

CIA wanted a powerful 'super' drug to survive. They looked around and found an all-in-all remedy.

Anti-terrorism!

❑

11
Terrorism

The definition of the word 'terrorism' given in the dictionary and the meaning given by the US are never the same. According to the US, one who violates, occupies, attacks others without any reason are all terrorists. It might be due to the thought that nobody else other than themselves can perform such actions.

CIA noticed that terrorism was spreading all over the world even before the downfall of the Soviet Union. They understood that it might turn into a headache for them. Technology was also improving. CIA got alerted that if terrorists too get the same instruments, devices and weapons similar to them, only guerrilla war will remain in the world.

It was known to everybody that the US was a rich country and it had a superpower identity. The wealthy nation would face more crises. Moreover, CIA was spying all the world without a tiny gap. If the US did not threaten anybody who worked against them, they would not be satisfied.

So CIA considered the fact that several groups who were irritated with them might turn their weapons against the US. They started to think about what to do to avoid such a situation. Counter-Terrorism Centre was formed within CIA in 1986. Their responsibility was to analyse the terrorist groups formed all over the world, their supporters, their mission and their targets.

CIA had already created an image for itself that they spy on the world only to control the production of dangerous weapons. The new branch was a continuation of the same. They started to find terrorists just like dangerous weapons and to remove them.

CIA had already created an image for itself that they spy on the world only to control the production of dangerous weapons. The new branch was a continuation of the same. They started to find terrorists just like dangerous weapons and to remove them.

CIA already had the human and technological resources needed. They just found a new goal then, nothing else. CIA's policy was to be at a step above the advanced technology. Although they rely upon human agents and spies, they understood that only when empowered with technology they can perform better.

CIA was using satellites worth several billion dollars at that time. They had several equipment which can be used to look at both the sky and under water. CIA managed to have eyes all over the world. They were able to monitor everything including your terrace, roads, bridges, military actions, scientific researches, terrorist activities and drug trafficking.

These satellites brought in thousands of pictures each day. CIA had a separate department named National Photographic Interpretation Centre (NPIC) just to analyse these pictures. It was a department which was formed initially to identify the Soviet Union's weaponry research. They used to analyse the pictures sent by the spy cameras and satellites in different angles using a magnifying glass.

CIA interrupts several offices and their telephonic connections all over the world. They get to know about the secret conversations, invasion plans and everything upfront. To avoid this, many leaders like Fidel Castro avoid discussing important matters through telephone. In many other offices, special places where eavesdropping cannot be done are constructed.

The quantity of the pictures increased later and computer software was used to analyse them. Do not underestimate on what could be analysed using the photographs alone. There were many experts inside the CIA who were capable of identifying the approximate population of a city, structures of houses, cultural methods and whether it is an industrial or a residential area based on a few pictures.

In addition to that, if infrared beams are utilised properly, several other information can be obtained from the same pictures. The CIA can correctly guess what would have happened just 'before' those pictures were taken. What if those visual images misled them?

For that purpose, CIA gathers audio messages too. They eavesdrop on important offices in all the prominent countries without differentiating between friends, enemies, rogues or silent countries. CIA interrupts several offices and their telephonic connections all over the world. They get to know about the secret conversations, invasion plans and everything upfront.

To avoid this, many leaders like Fidel Castro avoid discussing important matters through telephone. In many other offices, special places where eavesdropping cannot be done are constructed. But the CIA does not get discouraged by that. They keep on researching to find an alternative to gather information from everywhere.

They have formed a separate science–technology wing named 'The Directorate of Science and Technology' to produce the special equipment and devices needed for the CIA agents and spies.

Numerous media show James Bond 007's image while referring to the CIA or they play Bond movie's theme music. CIA did not like that image. Many directors of CIA have announced not to believe everything we see in the detective stories or movies.

In truth, CIA's science wing is inventing far more advanced technologies than those pictured in the James Bond movies. But, if this information is leaked out, it might affect the intelligence activities. So, they do not reveal their inventions. Their inventory list is a long one including eavesdropping bugs which can be fixed secretly, cameras, dark-vision electronic devices, various outfits, disguises and papers to write secret messages.

Another major goal of this research wing is to make secret compartments in the products which we use every day. For example, they would have made a tiny compartment within a small pen to hide secret information. It would look like an ordinary pen on the outside, but CIA agents can smuggle information through it.

Another major goal of this research wing is to make secret compartments in the products which we use every day. For example, they would have made a tiny compartment within a small pen to hide secret information. It would look like an ordinary pen on the outside, but CIA agents can smuggle information through it.

Not only pen, look at your surroundings. CIA can create a secret compartment in almost anything that we see around and smuggle information through that. The information gathered by the CIA are transferred mainly through this technique.

CIA remains the top organisation in this aspect. Nobody can beat them in spending huge amounts of money for secret research. They have several technologies which cannot be accessed by anyone. Most of these are designed and produced by CIA internally. Only on rare occasions are outsiders included in the production.

The gadgets produced are sent to the CIA agents all over the world. After that, all the information can be obtained according to their needs. Apart from the research wing, CIA has a printing office too. Starting from top secrets to blatant lies, everything gets printed in it.

If they have to spread quotes supporting America in any of the countries, they print the materials needed in their printing press. Small and big books on many important topics are printed here including the president's PDB reports.

Apart from these, the chief task of the CIA's press is to prepare fake documents. They print fake identity cards and certificates to CIA officers and agents who work abroad. CIA officers who start with complete homework start to monitor politicians, rulers, military people and the opposing groups at the beginning. Later, their circle expands to include scientific research, space research and drug trafficking.

CIA gathered data about all the groups who are involved in terrorist activities against the US. The gathered data will be given to the American government. The government decides on how and where to use the information and how to react to the threats. In many such situations, CIA's name does not get revealed in any of the actions. They just convey the message and carry on with their work.

After the anti-terrorism wing was formed, CIA agents started to gather information about the movements of terrorist groups in each country. Their major concern was to find out if any of them might be a threat to the US. CIA gathered data about all the groups who are involved in terrorist activities against the US. The gathered data will be given to the American government. The government decides on how and where to use the information and how to react to the threats.

In many such situations, CIA's name does not get revealed in any of the actions. They just convey the message and carry on with their work.

So, US people did not get the image that CIA really works against terrorism. They just thought that CIA only gathered information. Nobody knew the importance of CIA then. In general, Americans think that the world revolves around them. They do not bother with anything that doesn't benefit them. They just ignore it as if it will not affect the US in any way. So they did not realise that terrorism which was becoming global in the nineties, might affect them too. Even CIA's terrorism wing considered terrorism as an alternative to the Soviet Union.

Almost during the same period, several terrorist groups began to form in Central Eastern countries and were gaining strength. CIA noticed that. But they ignored them as they did not pose any immediate threat. These ignored people posed as a giant threat to the US in later years. The US started to take the anti-terrorism weapon into their hands only after that.

An incident occurred in the starting of the nineties which acted as a trailer for everything. Iraq's President Saddam Hussain decided to invade its neighbouring tiny nation Kuwait. The US was already familiar with Saddam Hussain. The US supported Iraq during the Iran–Iraq war. But the CIA did not trust Saddam Hussain completely. They had infiltrated Iraq as usual. They were spying upon everything that was happening inside the country.

CIA had understood the functionalities of Iraq's military accurately. They managed to gather information including the weapons available in Iraq, their trajectory, their capacity, the location of their weapon manufacturing unit and their collection point. CIA continued their observation even after the war to know about their next step of action. They noticed a disturbing feature then.

> *Iraq's weaponry strength was increasing gradually, not only in quantity but also in its capacity. CIA reported that they were producing weapons which can attack from a longer distance. At that point, the US considered it to be data when they received the information. They were bothered by it only when Iraq turned their target towards the US.*

Iraq's weaponry strength was increasing gradually, not only in quantity but also in its capacity. CIA reported that they were producing weapons which can attack from a longer distance.

At that point, the US considered it to be data when they received the information. They were bothered by it only when Iraq turned their target towards the US. CIA hastened its intelligence activities inside Iraq just by chance. They started to gather accurate information about their activities down to every second.

In addition to that, CIA gathered information about the conversations between Saddam Hussain and his supporters both within their buildings and outside, their relationship with other countries and who might support or oppose them if a crisis occurs. While compiling that information, they understood something clearly—Saddam Hussain was not to be underestimated.

Saddam's speech had a spark in it. He did not have respect or fear towards anybody. In any situation, he just checked if it would favour his country and himself. If not, he did not bother to make them enemies.

Nobody had the guts to inform CIA that America too had similar characteristics. So, they just informed their head office that Saddam Hussain was trying to become a superpower. George Bush who was the former director of CIA, was the US vice president. He already knew everything about Saddam Hussain. He guessed who was Saddam, how he was and what he was capable of with the expertise of an intelligence officer.

So he went to President Ronald Reagan and warned him, "Do not trust Saddam."

It was not sure how far Reagan took that warning into consideration, but the US was satisfied that Saddam was not a threat to them then.

From the beginning of 1990, Iraq's military activities started to become suspicious. CIA suspected that Saddam had a specific plan and for that he was accumulating his troops at particular points. They understood that Saddam would not do anything without a reason from their surveillance of so many years. So, they started to monitor Iraq's military activities with care.

From the beginning of 1990, Iraq's military activities started to become suspicious. CIA suspected that Saddam had a specific plan and for that he was accumulating his troops at particular points. They understood that Saddam would not do anything without a reason from their surveillance of so many years. So, they started to monitor Iraq's military activities with care.

The Iraqi military was building its strength along the Kuwait border. CIA quoted that and sent the report to the US that Saddam might attack Kuwait. Kuwait was an US-supportive nation from the beginning. Moreover, if Iraq invaded Kuwait, the US might face economic losses.

So, the US decided to step in. George Bush was the president of the US after Reagan. He sent a message to Saddam Hussain through the American embassy: 'Let us solve all the issues you have with Kuwait amicably. Please do not take military action.'

Saddam would not have minded even if the US had sent a threatening message similar to 'Do not dare to attack Kuwait!' He replied carelessly, "Who said that I am planning to invade Kuwait? That is rubbish."

But everybody knew that it was a lie. CIA sent the message that Iraq might enter Kuwait within the next twenty-four hours. Kuwait was a tiny country. If Saddam wanted to conquer it, a small army would have been enough. But thousands of Iraqi troops surrounded the country.

Iraqi Army captured Kuwait on 1 August 1990. Saddam Hussain declared Kuwait to be a part of Iraq.

The US could not sit and watch any longer. They entered the war.

Several kinds of missiles like Scud and Patriot flew in the Gulf War. The US Army was the hero in it. As usual, CIA was pushed behind the screen to assist them. But CIA's role was prominent in the Gulf War. US President George Bush accepted it frankly at the end of the war.

Even the Almighty would not have known what Saddam Hussain and the Iraqi Army would have done next. But the CIA somehow smelled their every move and sent information to the US. The satellite images taken within Iraq were revolving inside the CIA headquarters, 24x7. They utilised their agents, spies and advanced technology to send up-to-date information to the American government and the military.

Before that, CIA's headquarters used to create just one or sometimes two reports a day. Not more than that. But during the Gulf War, reports were sent every hour. The US was able to know what happened in Iraq like a live cricket match.

The major reason for that accomplishment was that CIA's network was well penetrated in Iraq even before Saddam Hussain's targeted Kuwait. CIA which was closely monitoring Saddam Hussain for several years, war able to predict his next step easily.

Due to this forecast, the US got all the information from the movement of the Iraqi infantry to the location of places where tanks, missiles and others weapons were manufactured. It was easy for the US to find each and demolish them.

CIA's another major task during the Gulf War was that it monitored who came to aid Saddam Hussain. There were two kinds. The first were those who declared openly, 'Saddam Hussain's way is the best. So, we will follow him' and sent their army to support him. This kind of support was obvious. The second aid were the most dangerous one—they were those who found out Iraq's enemies and attacked them unexpectedly.

There were many who were ready to provide Saddam Hussain with the second kind of support. Terrorist groups from many nations were ready to do guerrillas attack on the US and its friendly countries.

The CIA's 'Anti-terrorism' squad took care of them. They predicted more than hundred such attacks with the help of their intelligence wing and stopped them with the help of the rulers of that particular country. Without the CIA, the US would not have expected such attacks and avoided them.

Because of that, all the reports at the end of the war appreciated the CIA. Except in a very few instances, all the information gathered by the CIA during the Gulf War was accurate. The most important of them all is that the CIA smelled that Iraq was planning to invade Kuwait and reported it. It gave US a good opportunity to clarify their political stance.

Because of that, all the reports at the end of the war appreciated the CIA. Except in a very few instances, all the information gathered by the CIA during the Gulf War was accurate. The most important of them all is that the CIA smelled that Iraq was planning to invade Kuwait and reported it. It gave US a good opportunity to clarify their political stance.

CIA's contribution in the US victory was major as they had collected all the information during the war including military details and the attacks by terrorist groups. Although it was new for the CIA in gathering information during a live war, they managed their responsibility with care and earned a reputation.

But everything lasted only for a few days. Once the Gulf War's memories started to vanish from people's minds, they started to question the need for CIA again.

"My dear people, it doesn't mean that we do not have any enemies after the Soviet Union. We are gathering information about the terrorist groups, and their activities from all over the world. We are making sure that the US is protected by stopping their activities," said the CIA.

But people did not trust the CIA. They believed that they were wasting people's money and time by monitoring a few non-important organisations. Fortunately, President George Bush was aware of the need of CIA. He understood the importance of stopping terrorism. He wanted to make use of it properly.

So, the CIA did not face any immediate danger. They monitored the world as usual.

But what was its purpose? The 'terrorist attack' which they wanted to avoid, happened in real. That was the largest failure of the CIA!

❑

12
Not Safe

The year 2000 was upon the world and millennial celebrations were conducted in all parts of the world.

The US president received a secret letter from the CIA. It was not the usual 'Happy New Year' message, but a warning.

"We came to know that many terrorist groups are planning to attack major targets in the US. Five to fifteen major attacks are expected in American soil in the next few months. Be careful!"

What can the president do if he receives such a message without any preamble and which looks as if CIA is warning the US?

The president acknowledged the warning and continued with his usual responsibilities. The CIA had done its duty and was unable to do anything further.

It was not a single or two attacks, but five to fifteen. CIA had predicted that America was to face a series of attacks. But they were not clear about who were going to attack them.

CIA had information about all the terrorist groups of the world at their fingertips. Nobody else had such an extensive knowledge of terrorist groups then. They shortlisted a few as American enemies and sent information about them to the government.

CIA could not involve themselves directly in controlling or destroying the terrorist groups. They can help the corresponding country's government/ military/ police force by giving them information. CIA did the same. If they got suspicious about a particular group, information was sent about them to their home country and defence action was planned. A little too much precaution was needed in the matter.

CIA could not involve themselves directly in controlling or destroying the terrorist groups. They can help the corresponding country's government/ military/ police force by giving them information. CIA did the same. If they got suspicious about a particular group, information was sent about them to their home country and defence action was planned.

But, even after so many efforts, they could not find out accurately about the groups which were planning to attack the US. They were able to just speculate between a few groups.

American rulers are more cautious than any other country. Their caution reflects in every department of theirs starting from the police force, military, internal and external affairs.

> *Marwan was not a single person. He had a big team behind him and a strong background. There was also a leader who was capable of leading them. Osama Bin Laden! CIA had known everything about Bin Laden's Al Qaeda organisation, its basic principles, infrastructure, war training, army strength, weaponry and every detail.*

Can any of the terrorist groups enter into such a cautious nation and blast bombs? America's overconfidence made them lose their edge.

CIA knew that a huge attack was about to happen. But they were not aware of who would do that. Actually, they had that information too. But they failed to realise it.

In 1999, German intelligence contacted the CIA. They overheard a terrorist's telephonic conversation in Germany by coincidence. They informed the CIA that somebody was planning to attack the US. One of the members of the group planning for the attack was Marwan Al-Shehhi and his contact number was given. German intelligence gave the information and were content that they had done their duty. They expected CIA to take care of the rest.

What did CIA do? They noted down the name Marwan and his telephone number. They forgot the matter later. They cannot be blamed too. They receive numerous terrorist names, contact numbers and email addresses all through the year. How could they verify each and every tip?

So, although they received a tip about the group which planned to attack the US, CIA missed it. They did not realise the cost of their miss at that time.

Marwan was not a single person. He had a big team behind him and a strong background. There was also a leader who was capable of leading them.

Osama Bin Laden!

CIA had known everything about Bin Laden's Al Qaeda organisation, its basic principles, infrastructure, war training, army strength, weaponry and every detail. CIA had created a list on who might attack the US and Al Qaeda was a prominent member of that list. But all this was just general information. CIA did not know about Al Qaeda's next move and their methods until the exact date.

There is a difference between knowing if a person is black or white and what might he be doing at six o'clock, today evening. CIA missed in knowing that difference. They knew that Al Qaeda and Bin Laden might do something against the US. But they did not know that if they were the ones planning to attack or even if they knew that, they did not know about their exact plan.

Doesn't it look like stupidity? That was CIA for you. They did not tell anything in detail to the American government. They just mentioned that some attack was going to happen. Even after warning them, the CIA did everything to prevent the attack. But since they did not know who might attack, their concentration was divided.

CIA had almost fifteen years of experience in anti-terrorism activities. Their intelligence network was strongly placed all over the world. Information about several terrorist groups were gathered. Hundreds of terrorists were arrested. CIA claimed that several plots were stopped by them.

But, at the same time, a huge conspiracy was growing right under their nose and they failed to notice it. The conspirators were getting ready on American soil itself. Only a few knew about the actual plans within the Al Qaeda group. Osama Bin Laden had carefully formulated the plan without any hitches.

> *Information about several terrorist groups were gathered. Hundreds of terrorists were arrested. CIA claimed that several plots were stopped by them.* *But, at the same time, a huge conspiracy was growing right under their nose and they failed to notice it. The conspirators were getting ready on American soil itself. Only a few knew about the actual plans within the Al Qaeda group.*

In the past, during the Soviet–Afghan war, US/CIA was supporting Afghanistan. Osama Bin Laden was one among the several volunteers who worked for Afghan freedom. The US did not consider Osama as a terrorist then. They had classified him as a militant who was toiling to send Soviet Union out of Afghanistan. They were ready to provide him with any support then.

The Soviet Union lost in the Afghan war and evacuated Afghanistan. The US considered it a huge victory. Until then, the US and Bin Laden were on the same side. Only after the end of the war, the relationship changed into rivalry.

According to Bin Laden, evacuating the Soviet Union from Afghanistan was not due to any single person or a country. It was made possible only through the hard work and sacrifice of numerous youths for more than ten years. Bin Laden did not like the US celebrating the result of such a sacred sacrifice as their own victory. He decided that the US was not on his side.

Osama Bin Laden was brought up with intense religious fundamental principles and hence he was violently against anything that happens against Islam. The US did not realise that Osama would not stop at any point for his religion. So, they believed that Osama was still on their side. But, in truth, he had progressed far in another secret path.

Bin Laden's Al Qaeda was formed before these events. Osama and his group members had contributed much to the Soviet–Afghan war in its final stage. CIA was providing weapons and training to Osama's army even before Al Qaeda was formed. CIA helped them just like other militants even after the formation of the group. They were not given any special preference or attention.

But Osama utilised the opportunity well. He planned to use the techniques taught by the CIA on how to attack Russia's major cities, how to create political disorders and commotions against them.

CIA was not aware of Bin Laden's intention. Hence, the US too did not know about it. They considered Al Qaeda as just another militant group of Afghanistan. They calculated that Osama's group was Soviet's adversary and hence they would be their friends. They did not realise that Osama's resentment was not with the Soviet Union, but with the fact that they had invaded a Muslim nation, Afghanistan.

Osama Bin Laden was brought up with intense religious fundamental principles and hence he was violently against anything that happens against Islam. The US did not realise that Osama would not stop at any point for his religion. So, they believed that Osama was still on their side. But, in truth, he had progressed far in another secret path.

When the Iraqi President Saddam Hussain invaded Kuwait, Saudi Arabia took a position opposing them. So CIA predicted that Saddam might attack Saudi Arabia too. Saudi's king was terrified and asked for US's help. An arrangement was made for the US Army to protect Saudi Arabia until Saddam Hussain was defeated.

Osama who was born and brought up in Saudi Arabia did not like the arrangement. *Why should we depend upon others to protect our own country? That too US? Isn't it a shame for them to step upon our sacred Saudi soil?*

"I will take care of Saddam Hussain," said Osama Bin Laden. But the Saudi king rejected his offer.

Bin Laden was discouraged. He was troubled that the king did not believe him. Moreover, his major concern was what the US military might do to the country on the pretext of protecting it. A part of the US Army was stationed in Saudi Arabia on the Saudi king's request. They patrolled the country holding firearms.

During the Gulf War, Saddam faced numerous problems and oppositions in his own country. So, he did not attempt to attack Saudi Arabia either directly or indirectly. Finally, the war had ended. Saddam was defeated. There was no threat to Saudi Arabia from Saddam Hussain. So, the US Army should have been sent back, right?

But, just like Bin Laden predicted, they did not leave Saudi. They settled in Saudi and the Saudi king was also not bothered by it.

Osama could not bury his fury. He understood that the Saudi government was expecting more favours from the US and hence they were not bothered by their permanent presence in Saudi. Osama decided to act against the Saudi king from that instant.

The Saudi king was a friend of the US and thus his enemy too.

Osama Bin Laden who looked like a militant until then, started to look like a terrorist to the US.

CIA which was involved in anti-terrorism activities for several years did not attempt to control or stop the Al Qaeda so far. They just gathered information about them, but did not report them to the US government or try to restrict them with the help of the Saudi king.

Bin Laden had announced a 'death fatwa' against Saudi Arabia. CIA understood that his next target would be the US. From then, CIA started to observe Al Qaeda closely. Osama was not bothered by it and he continued his move against the US. Following the fatwa against Saudi Arabia, Al Qaeda released a fatwa against the US too. When the CIA came to know about it, it sent its first warning about Osama to the US government.

Bin Laden had announced a 'death fatwa' against Saudi Arabia. CIA understood that his next target would be the US. From then, CIA started to observe Al Qaeda closely. Osama was not bothered by it and he continued his move against the US.

Following the fatwa against Saudi Arabia, Al Qaeda released a fatwa against the US too. When the CIA came to know about it, it sent its first warning about Osama to the US government. The message sent through the 'first fatwa' was a direct one. Al Qaeda warned the US forces to evacuate Saudi Arabia. If they failed to do so, they were threatened to be removed by them.

The US laughed out loud on reading it. They mocked that a hidden group with no proper identity was threatening to remove their forces from Saudi Arabia. Moreover, only those experts who have learnt Islamic Sharia properly could release a 'fatwa' when the rules are violated. So US concluded that the ones released by Bin Laden are not fatwas but just notices.

> *In December 1992, Al Qaeda attacked the US Army which landed on Eden harbour through bombs. Fortunately, none of the Americans were killed in the attack. Al Qaeda planned for a similar attack the next year. The location for the next attack was the US itself! Osama's target was the World Trade Centre buildings at the New York city. On 26 February 1993, a powerful bomb blast occurred at the basement of the WTC buildings.*

Even then, CIA did not waver from their observation of Osama. They continued to monitor his move to Pakistan, the pressure given by Benazir Bhutto's government and his subsequent move to Sudan. It was the period when Al Qaeda's branches and brother groups were mushrooming all over the world. Bin Laden was integrating every group and was forming a strong network.

In December 1992, Al Qaeda attacked the US Army which landed on Eden harbour through bombs. Fortunately, none of the Americans were killed in the attack. Al Qaeda planned for a similar attack the next year. The location for the next attack was the US itself!

Osama's target was the World Trade Centre buildings at the New York city. On 26 February 1993, a powerful bomb blast occurred at the basement of the WTC buildings.

But, even then, there was not much damage as expected by Al Qaeda. Only a few were killed in the bomb blast. Moreover, the US found the few members who were involved in the bomb blast and arrested them.

When compared to the attacks made by Al Qaeda later, those two attacks can be labelled as amateurish or as a failure.

But, the US understood that Osama was not to be ignored, through the two attacks. CIA started to increase its scrutiny on Al Qaeda. The strength of Al Qaeda's network increased at the same time. A trusted inner circle was formed for Osama. All their plans were made in that inner circle.

CIA needed that information. Until they got to know who and when Al Qaeda was planning to attack, they could not use their intelligence. So, CIA tried to penetrate into Al Qaeda through their agents. They also tried to bribe a few who were in that organisation and make them their spies.

CIA had a few victories in their attempt. But they could not bribe anybody within the inner circle. So, CIA received just the superficial information about Al Qaeda as usual. They were not able to get the information about the actual attacks.

That was due to Bin Laden's diplomatic move. He had a habit of discussing all the information starting from designing an attack, who and how to achieve it with only those who were really needed for the plan.

Even inside the inner circle, information known to a person will not be known to the other person. Bin Laden might be the only person who would have known all the information and obviously CIA could not bribe him.

Bin Laden stepped into the next step in strengthening Al Qaeda's infrastructure after giving 'extra' security for their secret missions. Numerous youngsters joined Al Qaeda on hearing his aggressive speeches.

Only after that, Osama Bin Laden started to speak against the US. He released the next fatwa against US in 1998. CIA was not required that time to detect the fatwa. Al Qaeda gave an open notice stating: 'Be careful, US! America is a country which is against God. So, kill every American wherever you see them. That is the duty of every Muslim.'

Only after that, Osama Bin Laden started to speak against the US. He released the next fatwa against US in 1998. CIA was not required that time to detect the fatwa.

Al Qaeda gave an open notice stating: 'Be careful, US! America is a country which is against God. So, kill every American wherever you see them. That is the duty of every Muslim.'

There cannot be a more direct threat than that. Osama who threatened the US Army the previous time, targeted all the Americans then. Everybody including the army and public were a part of the threat.

What nonsense is this? What did the Americans do to Osama? Why should he kill them?

"All those who were born in America are our enemies," said Osama. He did not stop there. "Our war against US will continue in other forms," he warned.

He did not stop with just threats. Thousands of youngsters joined Al Qaeda. Several other groups also supported them. Intelligence data said that several of them had immigrated into the US under false identities. CIA received information that they were manufacturing weapons, bombs and even nuclear weapons secretly.

Osama's only goal was huge attacks and massacres on America. He concluded that Americans could be brought under his control in any other way.

Osama's only goal was huge attacks and massacres on America. He concluded that Americans could be brought under his control in any other way. CIA almost got the exact information about Al Qaeda's rapid growth, their source, the location of their camps and their trainings. But they could not know about the next target of Bin Laden who was hiding in Afghanistan at that time.

CIA almost got the exact information about Al Qaeda's rapid growth, their source, the location of their camps and their trainings. But they could not know about the next target of Bin Laden who was hiding in Afghanistan at that time.

Moreover, Al Qaeda did many activities to mislead CIA. They started to leak tips about many attacks which might occur in various parts of the US. Various names, contact numbers and addresses reached

CIA. Most of them were fake information or modified news. After the 9/11 attack, when the investigative team enquired about the messages CIA had received before, thousands of reports were submitted to them.

The internal conflicts within the two intelligence agencies CIA and FBI favoured Al Qaeda. CIA monitored Al Qaeda activities in foreign countries and FBI monitored within the US. Osama Bin Laden laid a road in between the two. That is, if they planned anything outside the US, CIA would find it out. But they did not bother about the movements inside the US. FBI did the reverse and they did not bother about foreign affairs.

The CIA who was looking at false information for a long time, lost interest in them. Even if somebody had said to them directly, 'Osama's men are planning to hijack four airplanes and crash them into US's prominent buildings' they would have ignored it as another fake information.

Osama Bin Laden expected the same to happen. He planned to carry out an attack at an unexpected time and in an unanticipated way. The day chosen by him for the attack was 11 September 2001.

There is no connection between CIA and how the 9/11 attack happened after such heavy security. But, how could they fail to find out that an attack of that magnitude was planned?

Al Qaeda's thinking evolved from planting bombs inside buildings to using airplanes as super-sized bombs. Since there was no precedent for such an attack, not only CIA, nobody could have predicted the way the targets were crashed.

If CIA was an expert in finding out secrets, Al Qaeda was an expert in safeguarding their secrets. Only a few were aware of the attack on America in Al Qaeda's inner circle. Even the youngsters who were trained to hijack the aircrafts and crash upon American targets did not know who else were involved in the plan until the last moment. The timing of the attack was also kept top secret.

The internal conflicts within the two intelligence agencies CIA and FBI favoured Al Qaeda. CIA monitored Al Qaeda activities in foreign countries and FBI monitored within the US. Osama Bin Laden laid a road in between the two.

That is, if they planned anything outside the US, CIA would find it out. But they did not bother about the movements inside the US. FBI did the reverse and they did not bother about foreign affairs.

So, Al Qaeda decided to bring a few from outside and slip in between the gaps. Their plan was to blast the bombs before data was communicated between CIA and FBI.

Everything went good according to Bin Laden's plan. Nineteen youth were chosen for this plot and were sent to the US individually. A few among them were trained to fly an aircraft and the others worked out daily and built their body.

CIA suspected a few among them. Until they were roaming outside the US, CIA followed them as they suspected them to be notorious. But, those youths of Al Qaeda cut off their CIA tails and entered into the US. Once they entered the US, there was no connection between them and the CIA. FBI or other protective agencies couldn't smell them.

At the same time, CIA started to receive many half-baked information. They came to know that Al Qaeda and its brotherhood groups were planning for some big attack. They were talking among them in coded language about the attack and were pleased that it was going to be a memorable event for them.

On 11 September 2001, Al Qaeda executed its attack successfully. Nineteen Al Qaeda youngsters hijacked four American aircraft. Two of them crashed on the WTC twin towers in New York. One attacked the US military's headquarters, Pentagon, and the fourth one missed its target and crashed in Pennsylvania.

This information was sent to the US president through the CIA's daily report. Although they could not pinpoint the exact date of the attack, they repeatedly reported that Al Qaeda had a huge plan.

But as usual, the American government did not take it seriously. They expected Al Qaeda to drop bombs on the American embassy in some foreign country or on the ruler of a country friendly to America. Nobody expected the bomb to be dropped on their own land.

On 11 September 2001, Al Qaeda executed its attack successfully. Nineteen Al Qaeda youngsters hijacked four American aircraft. Two of them crashed on the WTC twin towers in New York. One attacked the US military's headquarters, Pentagon, and the fourth one missed its target and crashed in Pennsylvania.

The US was shaken by the attack. They received a huge blow to their ego which boasted that they were the superpower and no one could touch them. That was Osama's expectation too. The minor attacks Al Qaeda made so far were just trailers. His dream project was the main picture and it was a smashing hit.

The US was more shocked than worried. Their peace of mind in believing that they were safe was lost. They started to fret about what might happen next. The shock and the insecurity turned into fury the next day. They pounced on the intelligence agencies. "A few young men have entered our country and attacked us. What was the intelligence doing until then?"

Since it was a local attack, FBI was targeted first. They were thrown stones upon for allowing the attackers to enter in to the US while failing to predict their attack and arresting them.

The next arrows were aimed at the CIA. Although the attacks were made inside, its plan happened outside the US. They were questioned as to how could they fail to find out Osama Bin Laden's plan.

CIA had already warned the government several times about the attack. How can CIA be held responsible if the government did not take proper steps to prevent it? Moreover, after the Soviet Union's downfall, CIA's responsibilities were reduced considerably. Their hands were severely tied in several affairs and hence they acted as just an information collection centre.

Although many reasons can be made, failing to know about the 9/11 attack beforehand was US intelligence's biggest failure. Only after this failure, the mistakes of other protective agencies began coming to light.

After the 9/11 attack, the US declared a war against terrorism. CIA had to support them in the background.

US President George Bush (* not the former director of CIA. His son and then president) increased CIA's budget and increased their powers. There could be several losses to the US after the 9/11 attack. But according to the CIA, the silver lining was that their importance increased again in the US.

Nobody is going to question if CIA is given enormous powers or if several billion dollars are spent for them. Americans understood that the country's safety is more important than anything else and realised the need for a powerful intelligence agency. At the same time, this understanding did not come out of their policies, but as an after effect of fear!

❑

13
Lady Spies

The room was full of enthusiastic youngsters. Each one of them had applied to work with the CIA. They were all floating in the dreams of interview and intelligence tasks.

From the morning, several officers addressed them and talked to them in detail about CIA's many wings and their functions. The fervent youngsters were mildly shocked. The CIA officer who was scheduled to talk to them was a pregnant woman. She started to explain about her wing with passion.

A lady officer in the intelligence division? The youth were dazed by the sight. The group which looked at her strangely were fascinated by her speech.

Not only in CIA, the entire world has the notion that intelligence division involves only men. There is no space for women in a spy's image with a sleek overcoat, hat and electronic gadgets just like in movies. But the truth is that women were a part of the US intelligence even before CIA was formed. CIA's founder Donovan was one among those who had a broad vision in his period.

Not only women, Donovan's OSS welcomed all the minorities like immigrants who had migrated to the US and orphans created by wars. The reason for the inclusion was not just pity. Donovan believed that intelligence tasks was common to everybody. So, he had a strong belief that anybody could be turned into a skilled agent or a spy.

So, starting from the Second World War, the US started using women for their intelligence tasks. They were chosen not for clerical jobs but as field agents. There are two kinds of personnel in the intelligence tasks that involves field work—officers and agents. Agents penetrate the inner circles of enemy nations and find information. The officers are responsible for selecting these agents and hiring them.

So, starting from the Second World War, the US started using women for their intelligence tasks. They were chosen not for clerical jobs but as field agents.

There are two kinds of personnel in the intelligence tasks that involves field work—officers and agents. Agents penetrate the inner circles of enemy nations and find information. The officers are responsible for selecting these agents and hiring them. These officers are called as 'Case Officers'. They operate mainly in foreign countries and their job is important.

> *Women in CIA were the most affected ones during that period. Even the women officers who performed resourcefully during the world war were made to move around the edges. Everybody acted as if their talents were not needed for CIA anymore. Moreover, a talk that Intelligence is men's work started to circle the CIA compound. So, for the next forty years, men dominated CIA.*

Many women held the position of these officers in OSS and then later in the CIA too. They were needed to act in new environments which had a different language, culture and habits.

The chief task of these officers was to find out who might act in favour of the US among the foreign nationals. They had to analyse those who needed money, how to make them work for them and how to trigger them. The officers were required to monitor the future agents/ spies continuously and understand them by talking to them regularly. They had to judge if the person was really talented, if he really had the guts to gather secret information or if he was just a fake. Only after careful scrutiny, intelligence tasks can be given.

Women in general had all these qualities. They are cautious by nature and they are able to easily guess whom to trust and which information is true and to which extent. So, during the Second World War, many women officers performed with accolades as OSS employees. Due to political reasons, their details were not revealed out to the public.

Once OSS was dissolved and CIA was formed, several women officers contributed significantly to the organisation.

But, since the war was over, intelligence activities were a bit slow then.

Women in CIA were the most affected ones during that period. Even the women officers who performed resourcefully during the world war were made to move around the edges. Everybody acted as if their talents were not needed for CIA anymore. Moreover, a talk that Intelligence is men's work started to circle the CIA compound. So, for the next forty years, men dominated CIA.

CIA's work was outside the US and they themselves concluded that women would not be suitable to go to foreign countries and take up the challenging intelligence tasks. So, the women who were working for CIA at that period were given just office work. All the other major responsibilities were shared among the men.

Many started to protest against women being ignored in CIA just like in other departments. Since CIA was a secret organisation, the protests were silenced soon. Even then, CIA women did not lose their hope. They stood their stance that women too can efficiently work in intelligence activities and get into field work.

The situation started to change in the beginning of the nineties. One among the few important women officers who caused the change was Jeanne Vertefueille.

Jeanne joined CIA as one of the low-level employees and raised herself to important posts. But you could not say so by looking at her. Nobody who looked at her could imagine that she was a secret agent. Her innocent looks helped Jeanne to a great extent. She spent her time in CIA's secret tasks without raising any doubts. She was a hard worker with patience and stability.

She was given a major task in 1986. Many of the CIA agents and spies in Moscow were vanishing all of a sudden. The reason for their disappearance should be that somebody was selling CIA's secrets to the Soviet Union. They had to find out the identity of that person.

When the US and the Soviet Union were up against each other, the spies in between had a good time. They earned well by reporting on both the sides. But, the task to find the traitor was huge. It did not look like a petty information exchange done by an ordinary spy. The Soviets were able to access top secret information too.

The team under the leadership of Jeanne, listed out what information were leaked out to the Soviet Union. They made another list containing the names of CIA members who were aware of that information. They started their investigation based on these two lists. It was like searching for a needle in the ocean, but Jeanne never gave up. She motivated her team and continued their efforts.

"The culprit should be one among us," said Jeanne. But CIA hesitated or feared to accept her verdict.

So, they gave her only a small team to investigate the issue. It consisted of three women including Jeanne.

The team under the leadership of Jeanne, listed out what information were leaked out to the Soviet Union. They made another list containing the names of CIA members who were aware of that information. They started their investigation based on these two lists.

It was like searching for a needle in the ocean, but Jeanne never gave up. She motivated her team and continued their efforts. The search continued both in the files and in the computers. After searching for two and half years, they got a breakthrough in their investigation. A CIA officer named Aldrich Ames was known to be spending a lot more than his income.

Jeanne based her investigation on this small tip and continued further. It was known that Ames's bank account had huge amounts deposited in it. There were no connection between his monthly salary and his assets or the amount spent by him in a month. By analysing all their findings, Jeanne understood that Aldrich Ames was their mole. But CIA did not have the power to arrest him and interrogate him.

So, Jeanne approached FBI without any hesitation. She did not mind that CIA and FBI never got along with each other well. She believed that a wrong doer has to be punished and nothing is wrong in working along with FBI for that.

So, a rare CIA–FBI alliance was formed. They started to work on laying a trap to catch Aldrich Ames in action.

So, a rare CIA–FBI alliance was formed. They started to work on laying a trap to catch Aldrich Ames in action. Jeanne crossed sixty years of age when the case reached its ending. According to the rules, she should have been retired from CIA. But Jeanne did not want to stop the investigation midway. She worried that if she retired, someone else might take charge and the accused might be released without atoning for his sins.

Jeanne crossed sixty years of age when the case reached its ending. According to the rules, she should have been retired from CIA. But Jeanne did not want to stop the investigation midway. She worried that if she retired, someone else might take charge and the accused might be released without atoning for his sins.

So Jeanne continued to work for CIA on a contract basis. She was satisfied only after proving the connection between Aldrich Ames and the Soviet Union with evidence and arresting him.

Aldrich Ames was not a regular person. He held many important posts including the chief of CIA's Soviet Union Counterintelligence wing. Americans were shocked at knowing that such a high-ranking official was a mole.

Jeanne took this complex issue into her hands, fought against it for years, got a life sentence for the accused and only after that, she retired proudly from the CIA.

Time magazine came to know about the issue and wanted to publish Jeanne's interview in their magazine. Jeanne hesitated at first and later accepted it. Many women all over the world might be hesitant and think that intelligence tasks are men's jobs. But Jeanne wanted to encourage more capable women with their ability to contribute to the field.

Just like her expectation, the interview given by Jeanne in *Time* created a stir among the American women. Many who were under the impression that women were just moving the documents inside the CIA, changed their outlook about women. This increased the count of female applications to join CIA. The count of female agents was just seven percent in 1990, but it doubled in the next five years, all thanks to Jeanne.

Starting from the end of the nineties, almost half of the new recruits of CIA each year were women. All of them have undergone rigorous training and have worked under challenging situations.

The problems faced by them are countless. Women in Intelligence have to face several off-putting attitudes starting from mockery like, 'Didn't you get any other job?', and confidence destroying like 'Intelligence is man's domain, what are you planning to do there?'

Even after everything, their job does not allow them to relax. They have to manage those who neglects or refuses to cooperate with them just because they are women and climb the ladder to reach higher posts. Apart from these, women working as agents in foreign nations, especially Central Eastern countries faced additional dangers. They had to perform their daily activities and fare well amidst threats, partialities and sexual harassment.

So, people assumed that Intelligence is not a woman's turf. They quote several examples of women officers who have resigned from their CIA posts. But, at the same time, there are several women who perform exceptionally well and reach heights within CIA. CIA emphasises American females to take those women as their role models.

Just like other affairs, the debates never end in this matter too. One group cries that women are set aside in CIA and another group says that it is not true. The only comforting news is that amidst all the debates and discussions, the count of women contributing to CIA is increasing consistently.

❑

14
Mirror Image

At a certain period, the CIA was suspected if any government failed or if any leader was murdered or if internal riots arose in any part of the world.

Many were under the impression that the US has formed CIA just to interfere in other's affairs. Likewise, CIA was utilised only to build US's 'Big Brother' image. With their secret activities, CIA and the US got more bad reputation than a good one. CIA's action in killing foreign leaders gained them hatred among Americans.

So, in 1976, American President Gerald Ford brought out an emergency rule. It banned all the US government employees and organisations to involve in actions that involve the murder of foreign leaders. The Church Committee investigation came in subsequently and several activities of CIA were controlled.

CIA's power limitations were clearly formulated in the law regulated by President Reagan in 1981.

CIA operated as a fangless snake for the next twenty years. They were able to perform with their old zeal only after the 9/11 attack in 2001.

Due to this, several questions and suspicions arose on CIA following the 9/11 attack. Did CIA know about the attack? Did they keep quiet even after knowing about it?

A theory prevails till today that CIA has hidden the information about 9/11 just to regain their importance. Although there is no evidence to support this theory, several believe that it might be true.

The reason is that in all the activities that US government took after the 9/11 attack, CIA has contributed to a great extent. Especially, CIA was secretly working on the US government's slogan, 'war against terrorism' for all these years.

The US government searched for Osama Bin Laden and his associates in Afghanistan. Later, they charged Iraq on possessing destructive weapons and invaded them. Saddam Hussain's government was defeated. Later, he was captured and hanged.

Go back and read the first paragraph of this chapter. CIA committed these activities covertly for a long time and the US government started to do them directly, that was the only difference.

Till before five or six years, 'Abolish World terrorism' was just the policy of CIA. The effect of not following that policy was demonstrated during the 9/11 attack and hence the US did not have any other alternative.

The US took a pledge: 'We will find Al Qaeda no matter where they hide. Those who help them will also face the same fate.' In addition to that, they announced that wherever terrorism buds, they will appear there.

The US Army started occupying Afghanistan with force. Their only goal was to find Osama Bin Laden either dead or alive.

CIA was operating in Afghanistan for over twenty years. So they searched for Al Qaeda's training camps, and hiding coves with the help of their agents.

But Osama Bin Laden was more of an expert in the Afghan terrain than the CIA members who visited the place on rare occasions. So, in spite of their efforts, the US Army could not find either Osama Bin Laden or the prominent Al Qaeda representatives belonging to their inner circle.

Finally, US exited Afghanistan without catching them. After that, till now, CIA could not find out where Osama Bin Laden is hiding.

But, could they stop their war against terrorism due to a small setup? CIA turned its attention to US's another long-term enemy—Saddam Hussain. After that, information about Iraq dominated in the daily PDB report which was sent to the US president. It repeatedly said that Iraq has possession of destructive weapons.

We may not be sure if that was an image created by the CIA or by the American rulers. But, the truth was that CIA had morphed into a shadow government and telling them apart was impossible at that period.

The US entered Iraq but could not find the weapons as mentioned by CIA. But they were able to capture Saddam Hussain and were able to dig out his old cases. George Bush junior tallied the calculation which his father could not.

'What next?' is the question that the world has now. CIA will be gathering and compiling information in that direction. If we are able to peek into their daily PDB report, we could find the answer to the question.

It was nearly six years since the 9/11 attack. During this period, world terrorism was growing stronger despite US opposition. In addition to that, the US had developed several enemies due to its opposing activities. The groups which they oppose are now more advanced in everything including member count, network strength, weaponry and economic background.

So, the chances of Al Qaeda or any other group carrying out another attack similar to 9/11 is more than before.

Hence, unlike any other time, there are more number of CIA agents who are roaming around the world now. They make sure that nobody points their finger at the US for any reason. At the same time, another change is happening silently like a mirror image. Terrorist groups are finding new methods on how to hide from the scrutiny of these intelligence agencies.

The US is not ready to analyse about their opposition. CIA's goal is not to find the answer for that question.

But the US cannot function without CIA from now on. They can sleep peacefully only when they are confident that their intelligence systems are looking at everything at all times.

❑

Annexure: Acknowledgement & References

Thank You: For my friends:

- Boston Balaji
- Ganesh Chandra
- Geetha

Books

- The Old Boys: The American Elite and The Origins of The CIA - Burton Herh - Tree FarmBooks - 2002
- The CIA & American Democracy - Rhodri Jeffreys-Jones - Yale University Press - 2003
- டாலர்தேசம் - பா. ராகவன் - கிழக்குபதிப்பகம் - 2004
- May-Day: Eisenhower, Krushchev and the U-2 Affair - Michael R Beschloss - Harper & Row Publishers - 1986

- The Terrorism Threat and U.S Government Response - James M. Smith, William C. Thomas(Editors) -SAF Institute for National Security Studies / US Air Force Academy - 2001
- CIA Targets Fidel - CIA Inspector Generals/ Fabian Escalante Font - Ocean Press - 1996
- ISI: நிழல்அரசின்நிஜமுகம் - பா. ராகவன் - கிழக்குபதிப்பகம் - 2007
- உஷார்உளவாளி - சுதாங்கன் - விகடன்பிரசுரம் - 2007
- 9/11: சூழ்ச்சி, வீழ்ச்சி, மீட்சி - பா. ராகவன் - கிழக்குபதிப்பகம் - 2004
- சிம்மசொப்பனம் - மருதன் - கிழக்குபதிப்பகம் - 2006

Articles

- The Ames Spy Hunt - David Wise - Time - 1995
- Afghanistan, the CIA, bin Laden, and the Taliban - Phil Gasper - International Socialist Review - 2001
- How the CIA created Osama bin Laden - Norm Dixon - Green Left - 2001
- The Largest Covert Operation in CIA History - Chalmers Johnson - Los Angeles Times - 2003
- 638 ways to kill Castro - Duncan Campbell - The Guardian - 2006
- How the CIA Works - Caroline Wilbert - How Stuff Works – 2007

Websites:

- http://www.cia.gov/
- http://en.wikipedia.org/
- http://hnn.us/articles/1491.html
- http://news.bbc.co.uk/2/hi/americas/3516233.stm
- http://people.howstuffworks.com/cia.htm/printable
- http://www.boston.com/news/nation/washington/articles/2004/07/24/cia_official_says_agents_have_infiltrated_al_qaeda
- http://www.fas.org/irp/cia/product/exdir_speech_051596.html
- http://www.greenleft.org.au/2001/465/25199
- http://www.guardian.co.uk/
- http://www.historyhouse.com/in_history/castro/
- http://www.researchchannel.org/prog/displayevent.aspx?rID=3688#
- http://www.thirdworldtraveler.com/Afghanistan/Afghanistan_CIA_Taliban.html
- http://www.time.com/time/printout/0,8816,982964,00.html
- http://www.usatoday.com/news/sept11/2002/06/03/cia-attacks.htm

Others:

- CIA Deputy Director for Operations Jim Pavitt's Speech @ Duke University Law School Conference - 2002

- Women in CIA - CIA Executive Director Nora Slatkin's Speech @ Chicago Council on Foreign Relations - 1996
- Women in the CIA: Problems and Prospects - Former CIA Case Officer Lindsay Morgan Kegley's Speech - University of Virginia – 2004

❑